CAT & MOUSE

ALSO BY SHAW COLLINS

CASSIA LEMON MYSTERIES

Cat on a Wire

Cat Dancer

Cat and Mouse

www.ShawCollins.com

SHAW COLLINS

CAT & MOUSE

A Cassia Lemon Mystery

GREENLEES
PUBLISHING

This is a work of fiction. Names, characters, organizations, places, events, and incidents are either products of the author's imagination or are used fictitiously. Details of any real life events mentioned might have been changed, including dates and people involved.

Published by Greenlees Publishing

For licensing, bulk orders, and general correspondence, see contact@greenleespublishing.com

eBook ISBN-13: 978-1-951098-25-4

Paperback ISBN-13: 978-1-951098-26-1

Large Print Paperback ISBN-13: 978-1-951098-27-8

Artwork by Kudryashka, Deposit Photos

Yada yada yada…

CHAPTER 1

Yawning widely, Cassia Lemon pulled open the white enamel pantry door and stared inside at the contents of the wide, packed pantry shelving—a space as large as some small apartments in New York that she'd see online with the headlines "World's Smallest Apartment," or "How to rent for less than 4k in the Big Apple."

Except this wasn't an apartment. It was just the space set aside for dry goods in her new home.

And yet, she couldn't find a single thing she wanted to eat.

Never mind the boxes of pancake mix (a newer addition) that formed their own column of goodness, the cans of pineapple and mandarin oranges sitting stacked behind them, along with boxes of more shapes of pasta than she'd known existed, along with a lot of other strange boxes with photos on the front, which was good since a lot were written in different languages. She recognized the Italian, French, some Greek, and maybe even Arabic written on some packages, but the Cyrillic alphabet ones stumped her. She'd have to do some fancy image search online to figure those ones out.

It was a rather strange and impressive collection of exotic foods for a mansion in the middle of nowhere Minnesota.

Not that she would ever say those exact words to the residents of Forgotten Valley.

Not that she had much chance either. Besides the party she'd had some weeks back, she'd had few people over socially. Just one in fact, Genevieve, who was due in about thirty minutes, and then Cassia's quiet morning wake-up time would be over.

Cassia glanced to the back windows of the kitchen that looked like a spread out of some architect magazine of rich people's houses: a farm sink, white cabinetry and lots of it, and expensive appliances. Outside, sunlight streamed over the bare woods out back that stretched off into the distance of her land, a thought that still thrilled her. Despite being nearly November and chilly outside, the morning looked happy and inviting. Genevieve would definitely want to go adventuring all day.

Cassia had to find something to eat, and soon.

But not from the relics that were a lasting reminder of the strange shopping habits of the housekeeper, Sarah, who used to live here. Or perhaps even of Cassia's dear departed aunt. Cassia made a note to check the expiration date of anything she pulled from the pantry in the future.

Just as she grabbed the right pantry door to swing it shut, having decided to go check the freezer for something quicker, a squeak and a brown flash caught Cassia's attention near the back of the shelving.

She froze and listened.

The massive museum-sized clock on the wall ticked away. Birds chirped outside.

Cassia gripped the fake wrought iron handle of the pantry door and strained her ears.

Nothing.

Sighing, she swung the door shut.

Squeak!

That was definitely a mouse. A cheeky one at that. Why would it announce itself like that when it had almost gotten away being unnoticed?

Cassia swung open the door and quickly shoved the items on the shelf off to the sides in big chaotic bunches.

Squeak! Squeak! Squeak! These squeaks sounded more upset and less cheeky. Well, Cassia was upset too. Her quiet morning had been disturbed by vermin. She shoved a can of stewed tomatoes off to one side just in time to see a brown tail disappear into a knothole of the interior wooden wall of the pantry.

It had gotten away.

For now.

Miss Mansfield's golden eyes blinked at Cassia, not amused at having been woken up from her nap in the sun in the front parlor. It had taken Cassia nearly five minutes to find the tiny black cat. There were more cat sleeping spots than places for Cassia to sit in the vast mansion. Sometimes Cassia felt like she was living in Miss Mansfield's house, and not the other way around.

Sitting with her furry black butt on the shelf of the pantry in front of Cassia, Miss Mansfield stared at Cassia.

"Not at me," Cassia said, pointing to the knothole at the back of the pantry. "Back there. A mouse. Go get it."

Miss Mansfield did not move.

Cassia grasped the small cat with both hands and turned the cat's body to face the hole.

"Meow," Miss Mansfield said, not amused.

"Mouse!" Cassia insisted.

As if hearing itself called, the mouse poked its head out of the knothole. Its little beady eyes stared right at Cassia.

Daring thing.

Cassia pushed Miss Mansfield forward to the knothole, but the cat was having none of that, digging in with her claws and resisting.

What the heck?

Weren't cats supposed to love going after mice?

Apparently not this one.

When Cassia finally gave up trying to force the surprisingly strong feline forward, Miss Mansfield turned her irate gaze from Cassia to the still-staring face of the mouse.

Cat and mouse stared at each other.

Cassia held her breath. What was going to happen?

The mouse squeaked from beneath the arch of its hole.

Miss Mansfield made a surprisingly high-pitched chirping sound in return.

Cassia waited for the wiggle of the cat's butt and then the pounce.

But instead, as if she'd suddenly thought better of it, Miss Mansfield relaxed and then stood on her tippy toes and *stretched* into a tall arch, her mouth opening into a big pink yawn.

A yawn!

The mouse chirped a short squeak. Cassia imagined it was a squeak of victory.

"No you don't," Cassia said. She reached around Miss Mansfield as if she was going to pull the mouse out of the hole by its whiskers. Of course, the mouse was much too fast for that and disappeared back into the blackness with a flick of brown fur.

"Dang it," Cassia said as her hand grasped at nothing.

Miss Mansfield stared down at Cassia as if she was a specimen under glass. The cat's golden eyes nearly glowed in the dim light inside the shelving.

"What are you looking at?" Cassia muttered as she pulled back out of the pantry and walked out of the kitchen in disgust, not bothering to help Miss Mansfield down or shutting the pantry door.

Genevieve's laugh rang out in the crisp air hanging over the expansive front lawn of the lurking mansion. Cassia still wasn't used to the scale of the place—three stories tall, and two complete wings—all for the personal residence of one family. And now for a single person. Her.

Despite the cold season coming on, the stubbly grass of the lawn still looked green, something that surprised Cassia, long after the trees had lost their leaves and the shrubbery had turned into scraggly collections of brown twigs. Not that she'd know what to expect in a winter, never having ever really experienced one in California. There, winter meant rain, unless one made it up into the mountains, and Cassia had decidedly never had enough money to be one of that set.

"*You* tried to catch the mouse? With your hand?" Genevieve asked, but didn't bother waiting for an answer before breaking out into more wild laughter. Her blue spiky hair glittered in the sun. The deep blue had faded out, leaving it more of a wash of light blue ends shadowing into darker roots. As usual, she looked incredibly stylish with a wild, asymmetric manga hair style and strangely cut clothing and heavy buckled boots. No small feat considering the lack of good clothing stores nearby.

"It's not funny," Cassia said with a pout. She kicked at the gravel of the drive where they stood by Genevieve's car.

"Oh yes it is," Genevieve said between laughs.

"That cat..." Cassia hesitated, then whispered as if Miss Mansfield could overhear them through the door and understand what they were saying. "She just *ignored* the mouse!"

With some effort, Genevieve stopped her laughs. She wiped

her eyes. "Well, I can see how she might be expecting you to take care of that too. Don't you do everything else for her?"

That was what Cassia was afraid of. Miss Mansfield had Cassia wrapped around her little paw. The least the tiny animal could do was catch any mice that showed up.

Or apparently not.

Cassia growled under her breath. This day was not starting out at all like she had planned.

And, most distressing of all, Cassia *still* hadn't gotten her morning caffeine yet.

"I recognize that look," Genevieve said, her lips pursed as she stared at Cassia. "Come on. You get your coffee while I raid your fridge."

"Raid it for me too. I've not had breakfast either." Cassia said.

"No wonder you're so crabby," Genevieve said as she pushed away from her old blue Honda that she'd been leaning against.

"I'm not crabby!" Cassia yelled after her, louder than she intended, but Genevieve just waved it off as she went in the front door of the Mandress Mansion. Cassia stood outside for just a moment before her need for coffee overcame her urge to pout.

"So, today's the day you get your mansion stuff?" Genevieve asked as she dished out a mix of eggs and vegetables onto Cassia's plate and then dumped the rest of the pan onto another plate for herself. Cassia had never seen Genevieve actually cut up vegetables and cook on the large and intimidating stove before. Usually Genevieve went for the easy things like chips or sandwiches.

But Cassia wasn't complaining. It'd given her time for two

cups of coffee. Plus, what kind of idiot would turn down hot food that they didn't have to cook themselves? Not Cassia.

No, Cassia was nobody's fool.

Grabbing the green hot sauce, Cassia poured a generous amount all over the steaming food on her plate. "Yes," she said.

"Yes?" Genevieve asked, looking at Cassia then at Cassia's plate. "Are you trying to ruin that?"

Shocked, Cassia looked up. "No, of course not. I love hot sauce is all. And yes, today is the day." Putting down the bottle, Cassia picked up her fork and tried her breakfast. Her eyes closed in ecstasy.

"Are we bringing it back today?" Genevieve asked.

Cassia opened her eyes. "Some, maybe, although I doubt much will fit in your car."

"Especially with a trunk that doesn't open," Genevieve agreed.

"I just want to see what is there, and maybe get an idea of what sort of truck to get for it—"

"Trucks," Genevieve corrected.

That sounded expensive. Cassia frowned.

"What?" Genevieve said at Cassia's glare. "This is a mansion after all, and most all the first-floor stuff was gone, as well as all the personal goods."

True. That was a lot of stuff. The mansion was so large it had wings of rooms, for crying out loud. Of course that would take a lot of room to store its former contents. If it was all there.

Cassia refused to think about how disappointed and heart-broken she would be if much of it was missing. It was entirely possible that the wretched fake-housekeeper-but-real-thief, Sarah, had dumped any goods that were not sellable art, since that is what art thieves were wont to do. If so, Cassia was going to have to have some very stern words for her, if she ever found out what prison they'd sent the woman to.

"Hey," Genevieve said, tapping on the counter to get Cassia's attention. "Eat while it's hot."

Good idea. Cassia nodded and dug in.

Today was too good a day to ruin with bad thoughts about bad people.

It didn't take long to finish up breakfast and throw the dishes into the dishwasher, a luxury Cassia still had not gotten over. Then they were off, cruising down the sunshine-lit road in Genevieve's faithful Honda with Cassia clutching the envelope with the single key and the directions she'd received from Thomas Rivers, investigator for the Federal Bureau of Art Crimes. He said they'd track down her aunt's pilfered belongings, and by golly he'd done it. Or at least had found some of them. Cassia had danced around the mansion the day the key was delivered by signature only from a courier service.

And now they were going to see what all that stuff was. It was like Christmas morning, only with a mansion-sized pile of gifts.

Luckily, Sarah had not managed to take things too far and the storage facility was only an hour outside of Forgotten Valley. Cassia was not quite prepared when Genevieve pulled off Highway 71 and headed for the fenced compound of the storage facility. Cassia had somehow imagined a dark and mysterious building hidden away, not some generic storage facility that serviced everyday people in the local area.

The nerve Sarah had had. She'd hidden the stolen goods right in plain sight.

"Do you have the number?" Genevieve asked, studying the directions for space locations on the board ahead.

Cassia checked the envelope. "Yes, 2010."

"Okay, good. To the right it is," Genevieve said as she

turned the steering wheel to take them down to the end of the long narrow parking lot fronting the complex.

Unit 2010 turned out to be one set of buildings over, in the middle of a row of enormous first-floor doors that all looked like they could be driven into.

"These units look huge," Genevieve said as she parked the car and they got out to inspect the place. Whereas the other side of the facility had many small corridors going to the back of the property, all lined with lots of little doors, this side had none of that. Instead, it was a solid, massive building with just a few enormous doors along the front wall. The spaces behind each door must be deep and vast.

In other words, huge spaces. Hope pricked at Cassia. These might be large enough to hold a mansion's worth of stuff after all.

The key Cassia had been sent fit a discus-shaped padlock on the pull-down door of 2010. Cassia turned the bolt and removed the lock. Genevieve swooped in and lifted the door, sending it flying up. Dust billowed out, forcing Cassia and Genevieve stumbling back, coughing on the musty smelling dust.

"I guess they didn't bother cleaning anything they stole before stashing it away," Genevieve said.

"I guess not," Cassia agreed. She blinked the dust out of her eyes. Stacked boxes lined the dim space, along with tarp-covered shapes that must be furniture and other large pieces. A small table stood in front of the masses of items, with another envelope resting on top, labeled 'Cassia Lemon' in hand-penned block letters.

"Whoa, a note. I wonder who that is from?" Genevieve said.

Cassia did too. For a moment, she'd had an irrational hope that the letter would be from her aunt, but that would make no sense. Her aunt had never been at the storage space. She probably had never known of its existence even.

With trembling hands, Cassia grabbed the letter and tore open the seal. The only thing inside was an index card with the numbers of three other storage spaces and three more keys.

Three more spaces.

"Holy buckets, Batman, we are never going to get through this all," Genevieve said in a low voice.

Cassia had to agree. Suddenly the vast array of goodies in front of them took on a heavier feel, like that of a boat anchor around her neck. How could she ever deal with it all?

BANG! BANG!

A sharp noise rang out from outside the storage space. Cassia and Genevieve jumped, then scrambled back deeper into the storage space in pure animal instinct to hide behind an especially tall stack of musty smelling boxes.

Cassia crouched. "What was that?" Cassia whispered. Genevieve shook her head.

Had it been gunshots? Cassia wasn't sure. It had happened so fast, and the noise dissipated so quickly she thought she could have imagined it. Genevieve's white face told her she had not.

BANG! BANG! The sound repeated, but this time closer. It echoed in a weird way that made Cassia think it was the metal doors of the storage spaces being hit.

Not a gun.

"HELLO!" a man yelled into the space where Genevieve and Cassia hid. Cassia's heart made an attempt to leave her body through her mouth, or so it felt like.

Cassia and Genevieve crouched in silence.

"I'm the caretaker. Who's here? Come out and show yourselves, or I'll call the law. No joking. None of your big-city crime is going to happen HEEERRE." The last of the words was punctuated by another loud BANG.

Genevieve squeezed Cassia's hand and then stood, despite Cassia's efforts to hang on and keep Genevieve hiding with her. Judging by the guy out there's attitude, calling the sheriff might be the right thing to do.

"We're just checking out our space. My friend's space," Genevieve called as she walked slowly forward, her hands up just for good measure.

Cassia looked down. She couldn't watch.

"Is your friend here? Because if they ain't, then I'd say this is just what we call *stealing*. I don't like people stealing from my workplace. It makes me look bad."

Cassia paled at the slight edge of hysteria to the man's voice.

"No!" Cassia said as she leapt up. "I'm here. No stealing involved. In fact, we're not taking anything today. Nothing to worry about." She walked out with her hands up. Cassia wasn't sure who she expected to see, but a four-foot five-inch man in platform shoes and a tight brown polyester suit right out of the seventies was not it.

His black beady eyes glared at Cassia over the soggy cigar hanging from his lips.

CHAPTER 2

The short man chewed on his cigar and stared at Cassia and then back to Genevieve. Genevieve was close enough to the door that the sun shone in her bluish hair, making it glow and look even more exotic than it normally did.

The sun was also heating up the contents of the space, and between her anxiety, fright, and the nauseating smell of the ancient boxes, Cassia's stomach started jumping. She put a hand on it to calm it. Now was not the time for throwing up, much as she might want to.

The man kept his gaze on Genevieve's hair and then looked down at her outfit to her outlandish buckled boots.

"What, is that some sort of Halloween costume? Bit late for that, don't you think? Also, you're too old for that," the man pronounced.

Genevieve's jaw flexed. Cassia could almost hear the tirade in her friend's mind going into a full-blown rage at the man's audacity. Thankfully, Genevieve also had full self-control. If Cassia hadn't known her so well, she would have had no idea how pissed off her friend was.

Hopefully the man was not so observant.

Judging by his actions so far, Cassia guessed not.

"Who do we have the honor of meeting?" Genevieve asked in a strangely choked voice.

Taking his cigar from his mouth, the man stepped forward as if he was about to start a lecture. "Owen Mensky. *MR.* Owen Mensky to you twos," Owen said, placing the cigar back between his teeth.

Breathing slowly in an effort to relax, Cassia nodded. "Cassia Lemon. This is my space. Or rather, it was given to me by the government."

Owen's eyebrows lifted at that.

"Some lady stole her stuff, and the government got it back for her. We're definitely on the 'not-stealing' side," Genevieve said to Owen, as if that explained it all.

He looked skeptical. He stuck out a hand. "Proof."

Cassia and Genevieve exchanged glances.

"Look, I've never seen either of you twos here before, and I sure as heck didn't rent the space to yous, either. I need some proof."

Luckily, Cassia had her letter from Thomas Rivers on the official letterhead with her. Cassia grabbed it from her bag and rushed to give it to Owen Mensky.

He swiped it from her hand. "What is this?" He pulled the letter from the envelope and opened it. Cassia winced at his rough handling of it.

Lowering the letter, he glared at Cassia and then Genevieve. "Is this some sort of joke? Because I do not like jokes."

"Clearly," Genevieve said under her breath, just loud enough for Cassia to hear. Cassia had to look down to hide her smile. Owen definitely would not take their giggling well.

"I repeat, is this a joke?" Owen said, coming to stand right in front of Cassia, forcing her to look down at him. Behind her back, she dug her nails into the palm of her hand to keep a straight face.

"No, of course not. Why would I be walking around with a joke letter?" Cassia asked, not sure how else to answer that.

"Wouldn't forging a US government doc be some sort of felony or something?" Genevieve said, daring Owen to contradict her. He muttered something under his breath and then pulled a jeweler's loupe out of his coat's inside breast pocket and bent down to examine the letter in closer detail.

It only took twenty minutes of Owen examining the letter with the loupe before he handed it back with a grunt and then stepped back and motioned for them to continue their work in the space.

"That was fun," Genevieve said as they watched the man slowly walk away back down the row of storage spaces toward the office centered between the two wings, leaving a cloud of black smoke from the now lit cigar in his wake.

She must be saying that ironically, Cassia thought. Nothing about that had been fun.

Or not much.

"Okay, back to business," Genevieve said as she clapped her hands, trying to break the strange mood brought on by the appearance of the rude storage space caretaker. Genevieve looked around. "Cassia, where are you?"

Cassia had walked back to find the envelope they had found in the storage space. She'd dropped it in their run to hide from Mr. Owen Mensky and had to squat on the dusty floor and retrieve it from where it had slid under a dark walnut armoire.

Keys and letter retrieved, Cassia stood with them in the palm of her hand. Despite the confusion and thrill of finding even more units to explore, her heart sank as she recognized the writing on the index card as belonging to Thomas Rivers, the art theft investigator. For whatever reason, he'd not sent her all four keys, but instead left the other three in the first space for her to find.

"There you are," Genevieve said as she walked back and found Cassia. "Everything alright?"

Cassia shook her head.

Genevieve looked down at the letter and the keys and then back up at Cassia. "Not from your aunt." She said it as a statement, knowing the answer before even saying it.

Cassia nodded. It wasn't that she wasn't grateful for Mr. Thomas Rivers' work, but she had still hoped for something more from her aunt. Cassia turned back to look at the stacks of boxes and tarp-covered items stretching into the darkness of the space. Perhaps what she was looking for was stashed somewhere in there.

There was only one way to find out.

A thump came from behind a wall of boxes to Cassia's right, startling her out of her thoughts. Her heart raced until she heard a grunt and a squeal of pain and recognized Genevieve's voice in the darkness.

"What are you doing back there?" Cassia called.

"Looking for a light," Genevieve said.

"Wouldn't they be by the door?" Cassia glanced at the wall by the large door. There were light switches there, but when she walked over to flip them, nothing happened. So much for the caretaking skills of the esteemed Mr. Owen Mensky.

"Okay, these don't work. I'm still confused on why you're back there?" Cassia called.

"Looking for an electrical box," Genevieve said, her voice muffled by the growing amount of stuff between the two of them.

A few more exclamations and stubbed toes later, Genevieve

gave a cry of victory, followed by the sound of a metal panel box cover being thrown open.

"Try now," Genevieve said.

This time when Cassia flipped the switch, the lights came up with the buzzing sound she'd associated with her short time working second shift in a shampoo factory. Why were industrial lights always so noisy?

Dust clouds still floated in the space, but the tarp-covered shapes looked much less ominous with the greenish fluorescent light thrown down on them. Now they just all looked like a lot of work. Was there room in the mansion for all of this stuff anymore? New furniture had already been placed on the first floor, where some of this stuff had probably come from.

Cassia looked around the room. Tarp covered furniture stood everywhere, filling nearly every square inch of floor space. The air whooshed out of her lungs as the scope of the problem came crashing down on Cassia. If she thought moving from California with her little apartment of stuff had been a hassle, this was like moving an entire apartment building. She sat down on the dusty floor with a little thud, hitting the ground harder than she'd intended.

"Are you all right?" Genevieve called as she came running back to the entrance of the space, yelping as she ran into boxes in her haste.

"I'm fine," Cassia said. "Just fine."

She was definitely not fine. How was she going to deal with all of this *stuff*?

Genevieve squatted down by Cassia. "Breathe. Come on, slowly. Inhale. Now exhale… slowly. Over a count of five."

Cassia looked up at Genevieve, startled by the commands, but did as she was told. A few moments later, she felt a little better. The dizziness she hadn't even realized she'd been feeling retreated.

"A paper bag works too, but we don't have one handy,"

Genevieve said as she turned back to look at the stack of stuff behind Cassia, "although it looks like we have everything else."

Cassia felt her lungs tighten up again.

"Oh come on, not again," Genevieve said, gently scolding Cassia. "It's only stuff."

Cassia had to laugh at Genevieve's look of consternation.

It was only stuff.

Several hours later, they'd located the other storage spaces, which, thank goodness, were much smaller than the main one, and from what they'd seen had only held dusty and some quite old boxes. Used to begging the grocery stores for moving boxes of all sorts of strange shapes and sizes, Cassia was surprised by the uniform and strangely tall, neat, brown boxes stacked in the rooms.

"Banker's boxes," Genevieve had said, recognizing them. "Not cheap."

They'd decided that those boxes might have been original to the mansion. Cassia wanted to go through those first, but Genevieve had insisted on getting an overview of how much stuff there was in all the storage spaces so they could make a plan. It was her one day off from the diner and she wouldn't have much more time to help Cassia, at least this week.

"Are you sure Trent was okay with me quitting the diner?" Cassia asked as she sketched out the rough dimensions of the fourth and last room in the small notebook she'd brought along.

Genevieve laughed. "Well, I'm sure he misses you, but honestly, it is about the same amount of work for me, considering how much help you needed with your waitressing."

"Ouch," Cassia said.

"Sorry." Genevieve did her best to have a straight face. It mostly worked.

"No, it's okay." Cassia smiled at Genevieve. "Thanks for the help. I know I'm not cut out to be a waitress."

"And now you don't have to be."

"Not yet, anyway," Cassia said. "It's weird how these small bank accounts keep trickling in for the mansion. Why didn't Aunt Mildred have a central list of them? Or just one gigantic account with lots of money in it?"

"I don't know, maybe because of people coming in to prey on little old ladies and taking everything they've got?" Genevieve said, pointing out that is exactly what had almost happened to Aunt Mildred.

"Good point," Cassia said. "Do you think Aunt Mildred knew what was going on with Sarah?"

"Maybe. Maybe she was playing along because she liked the company and thought she could outwit the woman."

"She sort of did." Cassia chewed on the end of her pen and thought about the note she'd found from her aunt hidden in one of the astronomy books in the mansion's libraries. Aunt Mildred had almost made it seem like a game, this business of leaving notes for Cassia that Sarah wouldn't find. Is that what you did to amuse oneself when one became old and lonely?

There were worse things, Cassia supposed, than being alone in a mansion.

"Hey, let's stop at the diner," Genevieve said as they rolled over the hill overlooking Forgotten Valley, Minnesota.

"Aren't you tired of that place?" Cassia asked from the passenger seat. She had the seat tilted back and her arm over her eyes. She was trying to ward off a stress headache from all the chaos today. That morning she'd thought she was ready to deal with all the stuff from the mansion, but she definitely wasn't.

Genevieve gently nudged Cassia on the knee with her right hand. "Just for a few minutes. Trent was gonna give me a check for some stuff I bought for Roger. This way I can hit the bank before work tomorrow. Besides, we haven't had dinner yet."

Cassia peeked out one eye from underneath her arm to glare at Genevieve. "You eat there every day."

"So?" Genevieve asked. "Isn't Trent an amazing cook, or what?"

He was an amazing cook. Almost against her will, Cassia's stomach rumbled at the mention of his name. Genevieve laughed and gave the car a little bit of gas to cruise even faster into downtown Forgotten Valley.

Forgotten Valley was a strange combination of early 1920s architecture in the old downtown combined with new modern amenities around it. Tourism drove everything. There was an actual five-and-dime, and even the diner where Genevieve worked looked straight out of the 1950s. Honestly, Cassia wouldn't have believed the place was real if she hadn't seen it for herself. It was more like the movie set for *Back to the Future*.

There were just a few cars parked behind the diner when Genevieve pulled up and neatly parked her Honda in her customary spot by the alley.

"Someone still here," Genevieve said. "That's a good sign for our dinner."

"Why wouldn't they be?" Cassia asked. She put her seat upright and stretched. The hour drive from the storage space was long enough to have nearly lulled her to sleep. Dinner was a good motivation to wake up.

"Tourist season is pretty much over, except for some stragglers over the holidays, but even that can't be counted on with all the snow and stuff. Last year Trent didn't have the diner open for dinner during the week. Only Fridays and Saturdays."

"Bummer for getting enough hours in," Cassia said as she got out of the car and shut the door.

Genevieve shrugged. "I don't mind hibernating in the wintertime. Besides, it's easier to get out for dance classes."

Cassia shook her head and turned away. Much as she liked everyone at the dance studio, dancing was definitely not her thing, but she had not yet found a way to break the news to Genevieve. Something for another day. Genevieve was a little difficult to say no to sometimes.

Genevieve pulled open the back door to the diner. "Hello?"

"Back here," a male voice called. Trent came out from the swinging doors to the kitchen, wiping his hands on a towel.

His curly dark hair hung in damp strands around his face. He looked like he had been running the dishwasher in back. As the owner of a very small business, he ended up doing a lot of the tasks himself just to keep the place running.

The rest of the diner was empty. All chairs were on the tables, and the floor still shined dimly in the low light from being freshly washed.

"Whoa, this is empty," Genevieve said. "And nearly closed."

"Yup. Winter's coming. The tourists are all home snug in their beds, or at least not here." Trent walked across the dining room to the front door and tested it to make sure it was locked. It was. Only the back entrance had been left open. "Sit." Trent motioned to the gold-flecked blue Formica counter. "I still have some cider. Hot even."

Genevieve raised her eyebrows.

"I'd been leaving it on for Mrs. Jenson. She just left, since she wanted to get some more yarn before the five-and-dime closed," Trent said by way of explanation. "That's why her car is still out back."

Cassia sipped the hot sweet drink gratefully, reminding herself to thank Mrs. Jenson for hanging out in the diner so much and getting Trent to keep the cider hot. She wasn't really paying attention as Genevieve and Trent talked schedules next to her. What Cassia really needed to do was think about the logistics of getting four storage spaces worth of stuff back to the mansion. Whenever she'd moved before, she pretty much did it herself, except for getting the occasional help with some of the larger things.

That wasn't going to work here. Or at least if she tried doing it all by herself, it would take the whole year she was supposed to live here to do it.

The one time she'd had some help was back in California. Ned had grumbled about being tired from working all day, but still helped her load up her apartment into the moving van. Sometimes she really missed having someone she could just bang on the walls any time of night or day and talk to. There were some advantages to cheap construction.

"So how did it look?" Trent said, leaning around Genevieve to look at Cassia.

"What?" Cassia asked, blinking at him in confusion. How long had he been talking to her?

"All your stuff? Or your aunt's stuff." He gave her an encouraging smile.

"It looks like more than I ever thought possible. I don't know how she fit that all in the mansion!" Cassia said.

"It was pretty well furnished," Trent said. He had visited the mansion once while trying to find a position in town and so had seen the place before Sarah had gotten her hands on it. "A lot of that stuff was really beautiful—at least what I saw. Between Ms. Mandress trying to stuff me full of cookies and her housekeeper trying to get rid of me, I was a little distracted. I don't really remember if much had changed when I went to cater there later."

Well that was hopeful. Going through all that stuff might

be worth it. Cassia nodded at Trent in what she hoped was a thoughtful manner, and not the sheer exhaustion she felt.

"You wouldn't happen to know of any moving companies I can afford, would you?" Cassia asked, not really expecting anything. Much to her surprise, Trent got up and went back to the kitchen, emerging a moment later with a business card in his hand, handing it to Cassia before sitting back down.

The card just had a name on it, David Clyders, and a number scribbled underneath it in ballpoint pen.

"An old friend from out east stopped by the other day," Trent said. "Apparently California wasn't his gig either so he's trying to start a business here too. I'm not sure how good he is, but he's probably open to negotiating to get a new customer." Trent leaned in across Genevieve to whisper close to Cassia. "Or you could just come back here to work to make some extra cash to pay the expensive movers."

"No!" both Cassia and Genevieve said in unison. Cassia was torn between laughter and being insulted at Genevieve's quick response. But she had to admit, a successful waitress she was not.

Trent held up his hands. "Okay, fine, fine. Just give him a call. He's probably more motivated for quick money than most of the locals. And he's got a rather, um, interesting new friend with him."

Cassia wondered what Trent meant by that, but his sly smile told her he wasn't telling.

CHAPTER 3

Cassia pulled open the door to Forgotten Valley Lawyers, LTD. The gold letters on the window twinkled in the morning sun. It matched her mood. A good night's sleep had erased the overwhelm from the previous day in the storage spaces and now she was just filled with excitement about what she was going to find in all those boxes.

Plus, it didn't hurt that nearly every time she came here, good things came her way. It was like visiting a fairy godmother or something.

A very tall fairy godmother.

Nate Perauski, all near seven feet of him, and some football player's worth of weight was scrunched behind the small desk in the outer waiting room that held Mrs. Anderson's avocado green typewriter—a desk that normally accommodated the woman herself. He hunched over the keys and pecked at them one at a time. Each tentative type with his finger was met with an authoritative slap of the electric typewriter's keys.

It looked ridiculous and endearing all at the same time.

"Nate?" Cassia said, interrupting his concentration. He

looked up. His face cycled through increasingly darker shades of red.

"Oh, hello, Cassia. You're a bit early." He tried to back up, but his chair was stuck on the carpeting and tilted dangerously back. Catching himself, he looked bashfully at her, then lifted the desk instead and moved it forward a few inches so he could stand up.

"Why are you using that?" Cassia couldn't help but ask. Mrs. Anderson was fiercely protective of her typewriter. She was also usually there, but apparently not this morning.

"Ah, yes, well, Mrs. Anderson had an emergency, and the printer is out and I really need to get this letter off in today's mail."

Cassia tilted her head at him. Why not email?

As if he could read her mind, he cleared his throat. "Has to go certified mail. Some things do still happen the old-fashioned way." He glanced down at the desk now sitting cockeyed in the lobby. "I'll deal with that later. Come in, come in."

Following him back to his office, Cassia was a bit sad to get away from the brilliant sunshine streaming in the large plate glass windows of the front lobby, but appreciated the calm and quiet of his office, as she did every time.

This time it was rather hard to be calm.

"So?" she asked anxiously before they'd even had a chance to sit down.

Turning, he flashed her a smile before he sat down behind his massive desk, looking more in proportion than with the smaller secretary's desk out front. "So, what?"

"What do you mean 'what'?" Cassia said. "Don't be coy. Do I get the keys or what?"

A series of emotions crossed Nate's face before he sighed. "I was going to surprise you, but you beat me to it. If Mrs. Anderson had shown up today—"

Cassia had stopped listening and stuck her hand out immediately over the desk in his direction, wiggling her fingers demandingly. "Keys, keys, keys…" she said.

"You are an impatient one," he said with a chuckle as he opened the right desk drawer and pulled out a fat, misshapen envelope and handed it to her.

"Twenty-six miles," Cassia said as she ripped open the envelope. "Twenty-six miles *each way*. That is how far I've been biking to get into town when Genevieve can't give me a ride. I thought I liked biking. No one likes biking that much."

"And how often was Genevieve not able to give you a ride?" Nate asked, teasing her.

Cassia didn't hear a word he said. Instead, she was examining the two key fobs and the neatly folded pieces of paper in the envelope. She looked up questioningly.

"The title, and your first six months of insurance. I took the liberty of setting that up for you. You can change it whenever you like."

"Did you wash the car too?" Cassia asked, only half joking.

He let out a hearty laugh. "I don't actually have the car. It's in the garage on the mansion grounds."

Cassia frowned.

"Would you like a ride home later?" he offered politely. Cassia couldn't tell if he was joking or not. Dry as his sense of humor was, he did surprise her with the occasional comment.

"Um, no. I've got stuff in town to deal with," Cassia said.

"And Genevieve's going to give you a ride home," he said.

"Maybe, but that's irrelevant," Cassia said, just managing to not sound petulant. At least she thought so. "Twenty-six miles each way is a lot of extra gas for her to have to pay for."

"Or you to reimburse," Nate pointed out. "Now you can just pay for it for your own car."

Cassia frowned. Another bill.

She hadn't really thought about that. She'd just been so

excited to have a car to drive any time she wanted. Sweet freedom.

Too bad freedom wasn't free.

Nate had tracked down a few of her late aunt's bank accounts for her. The woman seemed to think life was a gigantic game of hiding easter eggs, but instead of eggs, it was savings deposit accounts. It was only one step removed from burying gold in the backyard.

Cassia made an internal note to see about renting a metal detector next spring. At this point nothing would surprise her.

Unfortunately, all the accounts Nate had found so far only had modest amounts in them. Enough to get by and keep the lights on, especially since the mansion had special tax status in the county, but not nearly enough for the jet-set life she thought someone living in a house the size of an apartment complex should be able to afford.

"Speaking of which, have you heard from the people in New York?" Cassia asked. That New York law firm was her secret hope for a big payday in the bank account departments. So far all they'd been was difficult.

Nate shook his head. "Not since I sent the verification documents they wanted proving who you were. I'll try them again today. It would be good to have that meeting and find out what business your aunt had with them."

"You'd think the code would have been enough for them," Cassia said, unable to keep the slight pout out of her voice.

"Anyone could have found that card," Nate said. The card with the code written on it had just been taped to the bottom of a chair, but that chair had been in the remote master bedroom of her aunt's house. Not just anyone had access to that space.

Lines formed between Cassia's eyebrows. Sarah, the fraudulent housekeeper had found her way into that private space. Her aunt's paranoid ways had proven useful after all. Cassia hoped she got enough money to find out if she, too, became that paranoid. It seemed a small price to pay for tons of money.

"No worries," Nate said, seeing her frown. "We'll get to the bottom of it. You're very lucky that I like solving puzzles. Speaking of which, here is another piece." He pulled out a paper clipped sheaf of papers from the drawer and slid them over the desk to Cassia. "Another bank account. This time I verified the current contents. As with the others, cash had been transferred in and out on a regular basis, but this one kept more in it. At least enough for the onetime expense of moving."

Cassia glanced down at the figure on the paper. There were at least five digits listed on the balance sheet, just barely. Enough for movers, she hoped. Or at least truck rental and some help.

"This money stuff just doesn't seem right," Cassia said under her breath.

"No, it doesn't," Nate agreed. He leaned back and tented his fingers. "The goal of these big old estates was usually to run them off a trust, or even further back, off rents from the tenant farmers. There are no farmers, and they sort of did have a form of trust going at least for the taxes, but it really does seem like there should be more cash lying about."

The story of Cassia's life. Things looked great for a bit, and then took a left turn off into strangeville.

Cassia shook her head. No negative thoughts. Time to break that habit.

"Okay, thanks," Cassia said as she rose. "Call me the minute you hear from those New York people."

Nate nodded as she left the office.

Cassia shaded her eyes as she exited the law firm. She'd been early enough to stash her bike behind the diner and walk the few blocks to Nate's office. The sun shone on a perfectly blue early November day. It felt warm in the sun. She'd worn pants to ride into town, regretting it in the heat of the bike ride, but the days turned chilly fast once the sun started setting in late afternoon. It had only taken a few poor clothing choices and extremely cold rides home for her to learn to make good clothing decisions.

Or to at least err on the side of too many clothes. She could always take them off, at least down to the limits of decency.

Looking around, Cassia was at a bit of a loss about what to do with the rest of her day. Last night she'd meant to research some moving places but had been so exhausted that by the time Genevieve had dropped her off, all Cassia could do was feed Miss Mansfield and collapse into bed. She'd woken around 4 am to groggily take off her jeans and change into pajamas and fall back into a deep sleep, promptly oversleeping and having to rush around like a madwoman to make her appointment with Nate.

Procrastinating making the long ride back to the mansion, Cassia walked down the block to a decorative bench in the sun and sat down. She pulled her phone out of her jacket pocket and the card that Trent had given her fluttered to the ground.

Cassia bent down and picked it up. It didn't look particularly professional. Just the name, David Clyders, and the scribbled number. Weren't the numbers supposed to be printed too? And perhaps have a business name on there.

She stared at the card. Trent had said it was an old friend. If she didn't call, Trent might find out and get offended. She could at least see what the guy was like.

Now was just as good a time as any. When she got back to the mansion later that day, she'd research other places. Even though Genevieve had not taken the news of Cassia not going to dance class anymore on Tuesdays particularly well, at least that meant her evening was free, even if it also meant she also had one last long bike ride back to the mansion that evening. Dang it. Her legs hurt just thinking about it.

But starting tomorrow, she'd have a car!

Punching in the numbers on her cell phone, Cassia hit the green call button. It rang so long Cassia thought she was going to be connected to voice mail and was just about to hang up when a gruff male voice came blaring out of the phone speaker.

"What?" it demanded.

"Um, hello?" Cassia said, a little confused. Did she dial the wrong number?

"What? You called me. Spit it out."

"Is this David Clyders?" Cassia asked.

"Yeah, so?"

Cassia hesitated. This phone call was quickly moving to her list of recent regrets.

"What do you want?" David demanded when Cassia didn't answer soon enough.

In for a penny, in for a pound. Feeling a little faint, Cassia pushed on. "Do you have a moving service?"

"Yeah, so?"

"Trent gave me your number," Cassia said in a rush. "I don't mean to bother you. In fact, this probably isn't a good time. I'll just let you go—"

"Trent, huh?" The first hint of friendliness came to the voice. Just a hint, though. David's voice still came blaring out of the speaker as if he had one volume only—yelling. Cassia imagined the man on the other end with the phone held to his open mouth as he shouted.

Good grief, who talks on the phone like that?

"Yes, well, I might have called too soon. I'll just call you back—" Cassia tried to end the call, not quite brave enough to just hang up on Trent's friend.

"Nonsense," David said. "Where are you?"

Cassia hesitated.

"WHERE ARE YOU?" David asked, this time really sounding like he was yelling as loud as he could.

"Downtown," Cassia said so weakly it was almost a whisper.

"Downtown? Downtown Singapore? Downtown Santa Cruz? No, don't answer that. If Trent gave you my card I know exactly where you are. Don't move. I'll be right there," David said.

"No, wait, I didn't mean right this second," Cassia protested, but it was too late. The line was dead.

"No, no, no," Cassia said. She didn't want to deal with any weirdness that day, but it seemed the weirdness had other plans for her.

CHAPTER 4

"What do you mean he's coming here right now? Are you really ready to move this minute? I thought you wanted to clear out some space in the mansion and the garage first," Genevieve asked a dejected Cassia, who was sitting at the diner countertop, her head in her hands, studying the gold flecks in the blue surface.

Cassia looked up. "Of course I'm not ready. He was just so insistent." She lowered her voice and glanced around to make sure Trent was still back in the kitchen. It was the height of the lunch rush so all the tables and booths were filled with customers, mostly townsfolk enjoying a meal out. No Trent. "Plus, he scares me a little."

Genevieve raised her eyebrows at that.

"He was yelling," Cassia said by way of explanation.

"Maybe he's hard of hearing," Genevieve said. "My grandma yells all the time. Just because she's as deaf as a doornail, she thinks none of us can hear anything either. I have to put cotton in my ears before going to see her."

That was a thought. It was a much more pleasant one than David Clyders was an angry yeller.

"Hold on. I'll be back," Genevieve said as she saw a customer waving to her from one of the window booths. She paused for a minute and looked back at Cassia. "Want lunch?"

Cassia nodded. She didn't even bother trying to order anything specific. Both Trent and Genevieve had done their best to condition her to always order 'Chef's choice.' It helped Trent clear out the inventory, but better yet, it was almost always delicious. Almost. Brussel sprouts had turned out to not be Cassia's choice, at all. Not ever.

Once Genevieve left to do her job, Cassia stewed in her thoughts of how to deal with the unexpected problem of this guy. She didn't have the cash handy to pay movers today anyway. Maybe telling him that fact up-front would be the best way to get him to back off a little.

Besides, she was a researcher. She wanted to check out some other local moving companies too.

Still lost in her thoughts, Cassia didn't pay any special attention to the bells hanging from the door jingling at regular intervals. The lunch rush made that an almost constant noise

"Cassia," a vaguely familiar voice said behind Cassia, causing her to jump on her barstool. Turning, she saw a scowling black-haired, thickly bearded man with beady eyes, and behind him a tall guy with wavey beach blonde hair and a bright smile on his tanned face. The smiling guy waved at her while the bearded one stared at her with his arms crossed. They couldn't have been more different.

"Yes? That's me," Cassia said.

The dark man nodded and then thrust his right hand toward her, so close she thought he was going to hit her stomach by accident. "David Clyders," he said. "This here is my associate, Kai Huntington." He flicked his head back at the sunshine guy behind him. "Where is your stuff to move?"

Cassia opened her mouth, then shut it again without saying a word. She gingerly reached out to shake his hand but had only extended a few inches when David grabbed her hand and shook it so vigorously she thought he was going to yank her arm out of her shoulder socket. She quickly pulled back her hand as soon as he let it out of his grip.

This was going from zero to awkward way too fast for her.

"Well?" David asked, his tone almost a demand. "What's the job? We're good to go."

"You see—" Cassia started. Just then, Trent came out through the swinging doors from the kitchen and made a beeline for David. David turned his formidable gaze to Trent. Cassia could have fainted with relief.

Trent clapped David on the back and dragged him over to an empty booth in the corner of the restaurant.

Cassia watched wonderingly. What had just happened?

"You're welcome," Genevieve said in Cassia's ear, giving her a start. At Cassia's inquiring look, she continued. "I told Trent the sitch. He's going to smooth things over a bit. I guess David is sorta literal."

A voice interrupted Cassia and Genevieve's conversation. "Cool hair… like rad."

Rad?

Cassia and Genevieve looked at each other. The only place people talked like that was spoof movies of the eighties. Together they turned to look at Kai Huntington, who had not followed David and Trent to the booth and was now standing in the same spot staring at Genevieve's hair. Even in the heat of the diner, Genevieve's spikes had not wilted. As always, she looked exotic and put together, even in the retro blue waitress uniform.

"Uh, thanks?" Genevieve said.

"Are you trying to look like Kirito, or are you just lucky?" He said that like it was supposed to be a compliment.

"Who?" Cassia asked, while Genevieve said, "Ah, that would be a no."

"Who?" Cassia asked again, this time looking at Genevieve.

Genevieve patted her on the shoulder. "Don't worry about it, although he does have nice sword work. Good taste, my friend," Genevieve said the last to Kai before walking off to help another table.

That left Cassia alone with Kai. He didn't seem inclined to go anywhere, and Cassia felt awkward just turning her back on the guy and ignoring him.

"So, you work with Dave?" Cassia asked.

"David," Kai said. "He gets mad if you call him Dave."

Um, okay.

"Sure, no problem. With David. You know each other long?" Cassia asked.

"No," Kai answered.

That seemed to be the whole answer. Trying to start this conversation felt like pulling teeth.

"Tell me about yourself," Cassia finally said, feeling like an idiot, but it worked.

"I'm big into surfing, but David said if I came here and helped for the winter, he would show me the diggiest snowboard slopes. I'd never done it so said sure. Life is short. Seize the board and all that."

"Don't you mean seize the day?" Cassia asked, confused.

"Nope. Not the day. I need a board for any rad waves." Kai motioned his hand like a surfer riding the ocean. "Or snow powder. Plus, I can do it at night too, not just during the day."

Cassia put her head in her hands.

"Are you sure you want to do this?" Genevieve asked Cassia as she drove away from the mansion with Cassia blinking and clutching her coffee in the passenger seat. The sun was just peeking over the trees on the horizon and Cassia had not slept well the previous night, even after the long bike ride home. Rather than toss and turn in bed, she had padded down the hall and spent much of the night in the library looking for more clues from her aunt. Despite now having gone through half the volumes in the huge, two-story library within the mansion, she had not found one new clue. It only added to Cassia's insomnia-fueled crabbiness.

"Dave, no scratch that, Da-vid Clyders seems to be a bit of a loose screw, and his friend is either joking with me or totally out there. Of course I don't want to do it, but the price is right." Cassia glanced at Genevieve. "Plus, Trent recommended him." The silence after that statement held all the implied guilt that would come with not using David as a mover.

"I don't think Trent meant you *had* to use Dave. David," Genevieve said, correcting herself at Cassia's glance.

Cassia stared out the window and huffed. "Maybe. Well, there probably is no good time to move, anyhow. Might as well get it over with. At least we're not doing all of it today. Just a test run."

"Is that why you're providing the truck?" Genevieve asked.

"That is from all the nighttime news shows about fake moving people running away with houses worth of stuff and holding it ransom. The stuff in those storage spaces was all stolen once already. I'm not taking another chance," Cassia said, her voice gaining in speed. Apparently it had upset her more than she realized.

"That makes sense," Genevieve said. "How many times can the same stuff get swiped before you call it bad luck?"

"Luck has nothing to do with it. I'm taking a careful approach and we're ending this cycle right here."

"That I believe," Genevieve said and gave Cassia a wink.

They drove on in silence. The morning was cool enough for fog to have settled on the fields next to the road, giving it an ethereal look. Soon that would be snow on the fields, Cassia thought with some excitement mixed with dread. At least she wouldn't have to bike around in it.

"Thanks for taking me to the rental place this morning to pick up the truck before you go to work today," Cassia said. "And for promising to come help with stuff afterwards."

"No problem. I wouldn't want to leave a car in that parking lot all day either. Speaking of which, are you going to take me for a ride when you finally bust out your new car? Newer car." Genevieve laughed and patted the dash of her old Honda. By comparison, just about anything else was new, though Cassia did think the car she'd gotten the keys for was only a year old or so.

Cassia smiled for the first time that morning. "You know it. I'm just so nervous. I didn't want to try it this morning when in such a hurry, and last night I was too tired."

"You know you won't crash it immediately," Genevieve said, guessing that was Cassia's reluctance.

"Ha!" Cassia said. She wasn't going to jinx it by saying she wouldn't. She just really hoped she wouldn't. That car in the garage was nicer than anything she'd ever driven in her life.

Cassia sipped her coffee and imagined herself speeding along in her fancy white sporty car, the windows open and the sun shining. Of course, in this fantasy, her hair was magically styled, and she had a fancy designer scarf wrapped around her head to keep the wind from mussing with it, like an old Audrey Hepburn movie. She'd also have the snazzy clothes like in an old movie. All of her problems would just disappear because she finally had a nice car.

Or something like that.

"You missed a great class last night," Genevieve said, pulling Cassia out of her daydream.

"Oh? Have you finally asked Ricardo about social media PR and tips?" Cassia asked, feeling a bit guilty about ducking out on the dance classes. Ironically, she'd probably gotten more exercise biking home than if she had just gone to class with Genevieve.

"Some. Some. He's really quite good at it." Genevieve reached for her own coffee that Cassia had made for her and took a sip. "It got me thinking about the mansion. You know, everyone around here was always so curious about it. The Mandresses were so private in the last years there… for decades it seems. There was talk of grand parties there back in the day, but no one I personally know had ever been to one. You could probably open the place for tours and make—"

"No," Cassia said.

"You haven't even heard what I was going to say," Genevieve said.

"No. I've heard enough. I heard the word 'tour' and my heart shriveled a little and I want to crawl back into bed."

Genevieve snorted. "People are not that bad."

"They are not that bad when they are not traipsing around in my personal space," Cassia said with a sniff.

"Since when did your personal space grow to include a mansion the size of a city block?"

"Since last month when I moved here." Cassia refused to look at Genevieve, instead staring out the window.

"It's got to be better than waitressing for dollars. Besides, I seem to remember hearing about a six-hundred-square-foot space in California being your domain. I bet your front hall is larger than that apartment was."

The mansion's front hall *was* larger than Cassia's old apartment, but she wasn't going to give Genevieve the satisfaction of admitting that.

"The money is coming in," Cassia said instead. "Nate keeps finding accounts. And we still don't know what is up with the secret New York firm. They are probably sitting on a gold mine." That reminded Cassia. "Do you think this place rents out metal detectors too?"

"What?" Genevieve asked, confused about the sudden change of subject. "Maybe… not? It's a car and truck place."

"Right. I'll have to find a… metal detector place to rent from." Who did rent those things? Now that she thought about it, Roger the handyman probably had one stashed in his basement. If something was mechanical or technical, he seemed to have one of it. Or more.

All the things she had to do suddenly overwhelmed Cassia. She slunk down in her seat. Well, all she had to do today was to get the truck, get it to the storage space and survive a full day of David and Kai.

Oh my, what had she agreed to?

CHAPTER 5

And Mr. Owen Mensky. How could Cassia have forgotten Owen Mensky? How lucky she was to have him to add to her day too.

Cassia sat high in the cab of the old truck she'd managed to secure from the rental place. It had been fifty dollars cheaper to take the older one on the lot, and Cassia's frugal habits died hard. Even paying seventy-five dollars for a week seemed like an awful lot. So what if it didn't have air-conditioning? It was November. The manager also said something about a burnt-out headlight circuit, but Cassia zoned out on that part. Under no circumstances was she driving a huge moving truck at night. She could barely manage such a thing during the day.

So that was how she ended up with a twenty-foot box truck that looked like it was right out of the 70s.

What she didn't have control over was how she was stuck in the entryway of the storage space property behind a small white car with so much stuff hanging out all the doors that the car could barely move forward without dropping something. What looked like long sofa cushions hung out the back right rear window, a broom and mop out the left rear window, along with fishing poles and a half constructed cat tree completing the picture hanging out the passenger seat window. That, and the whole interior looked so jammed, Cassia was surprised the small plump woman wearing a cream dress with tiny pink roses could squeeze into the driver's seat.

The car was trying to leave, but it had a trail of things behind it—things that must have also fallen out the windows, or out of the trunk that wouldn't shut.

It looked like the adult version of a very depressing bread-crumb trail.

What made it worse was the woman was bawling, with her mascara running down her cheeks, making her look like a very sad and puffy raccoon.

The whole scene was bad.

And that was before Mr. Owen Mensky came barrelling down the driveway from the office building, yelling at the woman. Cassia couldn't hear the words, but she could see the soggy cigar wiggling in his mouth as he yelled at her, his spittle flying and twinkling in the morning sun.

Which only made the woman bawl even further.

Cassia couldn't take it anymore. She pulled the truck over to the side of the driveway, shut the engine off, and in the sudden blessed quiet, she descended from the truck and went to the side of the crying woman.

"Are you okay?" Cassia asked, peering into the car after having pushed past Mr. Mensky to see her.

The woman shook her head. "I just wanted to get my stuff…" the woman said. She started bawling again then, and Cassia thought all hope for understandable words was lost for the immediate future. The woman's light brown curls bounced like springs with each new sob.

"No, she's not okay," Mr. Owen Mensky said from behind

Cassia. "She is late on payments. She knows she is not to take anything if she is late."

Cassia slowly turned to face Mr. Mensky. She didn't know what her face looked like, but it must have been something because Owen Mensky actually slowed down his rant, and then finally stopped, instead chewing on the cigar vigorously while considering Cassia glaring down at him.

"Leave her alone," Cassia said in a low voice. She felt as protective as a Doberman pincher. Vaguely, she wondered where that came from. It felt very unlike her. And yet her.

Confusing, to say the least.

Owen Mensky seemed similarly confused, at least enough to back up and then finally turn and walk back to the office as if that had been his own idea.

Cassia turned back to the woman. "Can I help you?"

The woman shook her head. "No, no. Edgar is expecting me. I must go." The woman wiped her eyes with the back of her hands and then started the car again and drove away. Cassia watched her go, then looked back at all the household goods littering the driveway.

Walking resolutely, Cassia strode into the storage space grounds and picked up the dropped first item in the driveway. White and fluffy, it turned out to be a soft stuffed bear, something a child or a tenderhearted woman might keep. Cassia squeezed the bear and looked back in the direction the woman had driven.

The stuffed bear sat on a small pile of items arranged in the grass just outside of the open garage door of Cassia's storage space. She figured she could keep the lost items inside her own space so if she ever saw the woman again she could return them. She felt so bad for her.

It also gave Cassia some perspective on her own day. If all she had to do was deal with David and Kai, then that couldn't be so bad, right?

She held on to that hopeful thought the exact amount of time it took for David and Kai to knock on the entrance of her storage space. David banged on the metal door so hard that Cassia jumped and nearly dropped the lamp she was holding. She whirled to the entrance to see David and Kai walking into the large space while her heart raced and her mind told her to scream bloody murder, which thankfully she had the self-control not to do. After a few deep breaths, she managed to say hello in what she hoped was a polite manner.

"Hello to you too," David said, miraculously not as loud in person as he was on the phone.

Kai waved shyly to Cassia from behind him.

"That manager of yours is a jerk," David announced.

Cassia looked around, confused. Who?

"I don't think he understands this is a free country."

Huh?

Kai giggled behind David. Cassia stared at him.

"That little dude with the big stogie," Kai explained, holding a hand at chest height.

Oh. Mr. Owen Mensky.

Almost afraid to ask, Cassia did. "What happened?"

"He demanded to know what space we were going to. I was just waiting for him to ask for an ID." David puffed out his chest. "What does he think this is, East Berlin and he's guarding the border?"

East Berlin? What? Now Cassia was really confused.

Kai giggled again. He mock whispered behind his hand to Cassia. "David likes to watch World War 2 movies. They've got manly men in them." Kai curled his middle fingers in and then waggled his pinky and thumb in some motion she didn't understand.

"Like you would know anything about it!" David turned around and barked at Kai. Kai looked up at the ceiling and whistled a tune, seemingly unperturbed by the unexpected viciousness of David's response.

What a strange couple, Cassia thought. Apparently if anyone could deal with David, it was Kai. Nothing seemed to bother him. She wondered how much actually got through to Kai.

BANG!

Cassia jumped again.

All three of them turned to see Mr. Owen Mensky at the entrance.

Cassia was starting to hate that metal door. If she had this space for much longer, she was going to have to bring a sign instructing anyone who enter to not bang on it. Seriously!

Of course, Owen Mensky himself might be a bigger problem right now. He scowled dangerously enough that Cassia took a step back.

"What are you doing here?" Mensky said as he walked straight up to David, his face nearly at David's chin. Despite towering over Mensky, David treaded backwards until he ran into a sheet-covered desk and had to stop, trapped between the irate man in front of him and the furniture.

"I told you, I have business here," David said. He didn't sound nearly as blustery as he had a moment ago.

Mensky turned to Cassia. "Is this true?"

"It's true, and I'd appreciate you not hassling the people I hire," Cassia said, keeping her voice as level as she could. She was not usually confrontational, but she always seemed to be having to do so with this guy.

Twice in one day was just too much.

Mensky narrowed his eyes at Cassia. "Is that so?"

Cassia stood up straighter. "Yes."

Mensky looked at David and Kai, then back at Cassia. "There better not be any funny business going on here."

Her reserves of bravery completely cleared out, Cassia merely shook her head. Thankfully, Mensky was satisfied with his warning and left after giving everyone another meaningful look and stalking back out the large open garage door.

"Whoa, that dude like needs to chill out, bro," Kai said as he watched Mensky leave.

Cassia could not agree more. She exhaled heavily once Mensky was far enough away to not hear it.

David shook himself. He looked around the space, trying to play off what had just happened. "So what of this goes?"

Several hours later, Kai was cramming some boxes into the back of Cassia's moving truck, trying to get them to squeeze in while David pulled down on the truck's sliding cargo door. At first Cassia had tried to carefully select what went into the small truck—the truck small only in comparison to the massive amount of stuff in the storage space—but after an hour, they were just grabbing anything that would fit and shoving it in willy-nilly. It was like a reverse game of Jenga, but with much larger objects. Cassia wondered if the whole mess was going to fall out and crush her when she tried to open the truck again at the mansion.

Slapping a padlock on the now shut truck, Cassia turned back and surveyed the space. Kai lounged by the entrance, giving her a warm smile. Despite working hard for the last several hours, he had the same sunny disposition, which was good because David still had his same sour one.

"Whoa. This your loot?" Kai asked, hooking a thumb at the pile of stuff that Cassia had set by the door earlier. "Cute bear. I'd chill with him any ole day."

Cassia had forgotten about what happened that morning. That poor woman. "No, not mine, but I'm going to hold on to it for someone. Let's get it inside."

After everything was secured inside, and Cassia had paid David and Kai with crisp fifties she'd grabbed from the bank that morning, Cassia started the truck and set off for home. Nothing sounded better than a luxurious dinner with Miss Mansfield and then maybe a bath. She'd text Genevieve to not bother coming since it was all done, at least for now. Nothing else had to be accomplished that night.

Bang! Bang! Bang!

Cassia woke bleary-eyed and confused. She'd been sleeping deeply, but it was bright in the room. Very confusing. At first, she had no idea what time it was, or even where she was.

It took several blinks for her to realize she'd fallen asleep on her bed, fully dressed with all the lights burning brightly. A plate with the crumby remains of a sandwich sat on the bedspread, along with an astrophysics text on the galactic dynamics. Miss Mansfield curled on one corner of the expansive bed, her head upright and golden eyes alert.

What had woken Cassia, and apparently Miss Mansfield, up?

Bang! Bang! Bang!

Oh, the front door. Cassia was starting to hate banging with all of her heart. She'd heard way too much of it the last few days. Enough for a lifetime.

Cassia shoved her way to the edge of the bed and stumbled toward the bedroom door. Still disorientated, she grabbed her phone off a box on the way to the door. It was dead, the screen refusing to turn on. She normally charged it every night, but she must have forgotten to actually plug it in last night.

Clutching the dead phone out of habit, Cassia padded down the hall to the front door. Luckily she was still in her jeans and sweatshirt from the day before and didn't have to worry about finding clothes in her half-awake state. Away from the brightly lit bedroom, the entryway windows showed black outside. It was sometime during the middle of the night. At least the front stoop light was on.

Cassia peeked through the security peephole and then jumped back. Sheriff Andrews' right eyeball was inches from the opening, looking like a gigantic blue saucer looking this way and that. Cassia put her hand to her heart. Holy buckets —these people and their trying-to-stare into-peepholes ways. That is not how peepholes were supposed to work! It must be something in the water in Forgotten Valley that created this strange phenomenon.

Opening the door, Cassia didn't even bother to say hello. Even if she tried, she knew from experience that Sheriff Andrews would just blurt out whatever it was he wanted. It was easier to just to let him talk first.

She stared at him, waiting. Even though it was dark o'clock, he had his uniform on, looking spotlessly creased and skintight as always on his muscular frame. Did the man ever slouch out? Probably not.

But this time, instead of barking out his questions—or more often than not, demands—he just stared at her like she was some wayward child.

"What?" Cassia asked defensively.

He exhaled heavily. "Cassia Lemon, do you have storage space at Mucho Junk off Highway 71, and were you there today?"

"Yes," Cassia said slowly. "Is that a crime that you have to come visit me in the middle of the night about?"

"No, it is not," he said, pushing his hat back and rubbing

his forehead. "I'm here about the murder of Owen Mensky last evening. You were named as present at the storage space at the time. Do you know anything about this event?"

"Murder?" Cassia asked, shock running through her body. Suddenly, her entire body felt as cold as the handle of the door.

CHAPTER 6

Cassia gripped the front door of the mansion, staring at Sheriff Andrews as a strange feeling passed over her skin. Suddenly she felt chill and wanted to sit down right where she was standing on the front mansion stoop.

Sheriff Andrews must have seen something on her face, for he reached forward and put a hand under her elbow and guided her into the house and out of the damp night air. "Let's go inside and talk. We're letting all the cold in."

Nodding, Cassia followed him in. It was true, she'd just gotten the huge boilers turned on in the mansion a week ago and was dreading to find out what the gas bill was going to be.

She shook her head. How could she get distracted thinking about the heat when someone else was dead?

"Another one?" Cassia asked.

"Yup," Sheriff Andrews said. "That's what I thought. And of course you're involved."

"I am not involved!" Cassia said immediately. That one she didn't have to think about. At her feet below, Miss Mansfield meowed demandingly with her "food now" meow. Cassia blinked but started walking to the kitchen out of habit more than anything.

"Please come in," Cassia said as she walked into the kitchen. She knew Sheriff Andrews would follow.

Feeding Miss Mansfield helped Cassia feel a moment of normalcy. It was part of her daily routine, and she could do it almost without thinking.

Sheriff Andrews stood awkwardly in the dim white kitchen lit only by the under the cupboard lights as Cassia spooned the canned food into a white porcelain dish and set it in Miss Mansfield's special eating area.

Finally, Cassia put the dirty spoon in the sink and turned to face Sheriff Andrews. "I still don't understand why you came out here."

"Your phone was going right to voicemail. I'd hate to think you'd be a flight risk," Sheriff Andrews said gruffly, almost too gruffly. Had he been worried about Cassia? The thought tickled at her mind as she pulled out her dead phone from her back pocket.

She'd have to charge it as soon as possible. What else had she missed?

"I'm not a flight risk. Now what?" Cassia asked, deciding to face the question head-on. Putting the phone on the kitchen island, she stared belligerently at Sheriff Andrews. It was a terrible attitude to display, she knew, but it was late and she was tired and crabby. And really, she really didn't want to go to town for the dreaded questioning that she knew was coming, but sooner was probably better than later.

Then her curiosity got the better of her. "Better yet, what happened to Mr. Mensky?"

"That I can't tell you at this time. It's part of the investigation, but we do have to ask you some questions," Sheriff Andrews said.

Cassia knew it. More time downtown in that horrid sheriff's office.

"Can I at least have something to eat first?" Cassia asked. "Or coffee? You wouldn't be so cruel as to force me to go without coffee, would you?"

Much to Cassia's surprise, not only did Sheriff Andrews give her time to make coffee, he insisted she eat something too. She gave him the side-eye as she prepared her comfort food sandwiches of pimento loaf and mustard, mentally daring him to say a word about eating something like that at five o'clock in the morning. He looked stoically off to the side as if he wasn't noticing a thing. Cassia grunted but didn't comment on it. No sense pushing her luck.

He balked at letting her eat in the squad car. Cassia wolfed down one of her sandwiches, then shoved the second one in a plastic bag and shoved it into her backpack.

For a moment she thought about trying to drive her car for the first time into town, but the thought of the sheriff following her as she learned how the car worked (and probably messed up a thing or two along the way) was enough to dissuade her of that idea.

He also wouldn't let her ride in front so Cassia had to sit in the back. She hoped not too many people were out and about in town to see her arrive in Forgotten Valley in the back of the sheriff's car. It happened way too often. It *really* happened way too often for someone who hadn't even lived here that long.

Hopefully Nate was working today anyhow. Cassia had managed to get some charge on her phone while making breakfast and used some of it to send Nate a text on the ride in to meet her at the jail.

The sun was well over the horizon now and streamed into the sheriff's office, lighting up the paper-covered desk of Deputy Chester, along with what used to be a secretary's desk, and some tables lined along the back wall. The only thing that was pristine in the cinderblock box of a room was Sheriff Andrews' desk, where everything was so neatly lined up that Cassia wondered if Sheriff Andrews pulled out a ruler to check the placement of everything.

She sat in front of Sheriff Andrews' desk, with Nate, her lawyer, sitting in the chair next to her. Nate wore a neat suit and a paisley tie. He looked like it was an afternoon meeting and not like she had woken him up at 5 am. People who could do that in the morning always impressed Cassia. She couldn't even think clearly before 9 am it seemed.

Today felt like it was not going to be an exception to that. Nothing about this morning made any sense to her.

Cassia repeated her story for the third time to Sheriff Andrews. He checked his notes while she spoke. The questioning didn't seem to usually take this long. A bad feeling lingered in her belly.

As Cassia spoke, she kept waiting for Nate to tell her not to talk about stuff, but he didn't say a word. Maybe what she was saying was no big deal.

And why should it be? She'd been there to meet David and Kai. They packed up some stuff, and then everyone left. Easy. Simple.

No crime involved.

At least by herself.

When she finished, Sheriff Andrews set his pen down perfectly aligned to the top of his notepad, which itself was perfectly square on the desk pad on his desk. He tented his fingers and looked at her.

"We're going to need you to sign this when it's typed up. Don't leave town," Sheriff Andrews said.

Cassia nodded, too tired to even protest.

"She won't," Nate assured the sheriff when Cassia didn't speak.

The door to the outside whooshed open and Deputy Chester walked in. His big brown eyes met Cassia's, then he quickly looked away. Cassia always thought he looked like a gigantic puppy dog, but this time he looked like one that had just made a mistake on the carpet. Or someone else had.

Deputy Chester came around Sheriff Andrews' desk to whisper something in the sheriff's ear. Sheriff Andrew's eyes widened just a bit and he glanced at Cassia before he got control of his face again.

Sheriff Andrews pulled back and looked at Deputy Chester. "Are you sure?" he asked the young deputy. Chester nodded while turning red and backing away. He held a tiny videotape in his hand and motioned to a back room.

"Can you please excuse us for a moment?" Sheriff Andrews asked as he rose. Cassia and Nate nodded.

"What was that all about, do you think?" Cassia asked as Sheriff Andrews followed Deputy Chester into the room. The door to the room shut partway, but not completely. If Cassia or Nate made a move to leave the sheriff's office, Andrews or Chester would have seen it.

Nate shook his head. Whatever he thought was going on, he wasn't ready to share it with Cassia just yet.

Before Cassia could decide if that upset her or not, Sheriff Andrews and Deputy Chester came back into the main room. Sheriff Andrews made a beeline for Cassia.

"Cassia Lemon, I am arresting you for the suspected murder of Owen Mensky," Sheriff Andrews said as he pulled the handcuffs from his belt.

"What?" Cassia asked, shocked as she looked up. Sheriff Andrews wouldn't meet her eyes.

"Don't say anything else," Nate said to Cassia. "I'll find out what's going on." Nate took Cassia's bag for her without being told as Cassia was led away to the ancient jail cell around the corner.

"This has to be a mistake," Cassia said as the barred door slammed shut behind her.

No one answered.

She sat down on the sole cot in the tiny room with a thud.

Deputy Chester typed away at his desk around the corner from the jail. It was later afternoon and Cassia had mentally given up on her plans for the day and now lay sprawled on the musty smelling cot in the middle of the cell. The sun came in the high window to stream on her and the dark green army blanket on the cot. It was almost pleasant. If she was a cat, she could have just napped in the sun and forgotten all about being charged with murder.

Murder.

Another one.

No one had told her what had happened to poor Mr. Owen Mensky. Cassia wouldn't wish a bad end on anyone, but the way Mr. Mensky acted, she could imagine a lot of people who did have it out for him. Every single time she'd seen him he had upset someone. Sometimes quite a lot.

"I'm sorry," a quiet voice said, drifting from around the corner.

"Deputy Chester?" Cassia asked, pulled out of her reverie.

A pause.

"Yes," he said.

"Did you just say something?"

"No," came his voice.

Cassia frowned.

"I'm sure you just said something," Cassia said.

"Yes," Deputy Chester said.

What something was *he* referring to? Now Cassia was confused. Her thought muddled even trying to come up with the next question.

"You're right," he said. "I said I'm sorry. Sorry you're in there for murdering Mensky."

"I didn't murder Mensky!" Cassia said, despite Nate's admonishment to not say anything to anybody without him being there. She bit her lip to stop herself from saying anything else.

"Okay," Deputy Chester said. A moment later, the clicking of his keyboard keys echoed through the space. He paused, as if he was going to say something else, then the typing started up again.

Maybe he was feeling chatty.

"What was that thing you brought in this morning?" Cassia asked. She crossed her fingers, hoping for an answer.

A heavy silence hung in the air for a moment as Deputy Chester stopped typing but didn't answer. Cassia held her breath, afraid that making any noise would push him into ignoring her question.

But he didn't. Finally, he said, "A security tape from Mucho Junk."

A security tape! But what could it show that would indict her?

The door to the outside swung open, bringing in the sounds of the street. The sudden scrape of Deputy Chester's chair on the floor told Cassia that Chester had gotten up and gone to see whoever had come into the station. Cassia craned her neck to look out the jail cell door but it was no use—the cell lay around the corner from the main office space and she couldn't see anything.

Of all the rotten luck to have someone come in just when Deputy Chester was about to tell her useful stuff.

CHAPTER 7

Nate stood in the jail cell. Apparently he'd decided not to brave trying to lower his near seven-foot-tall body to sit on it this time. Cassia stood, still having to crane her neck uncomfortably far to look at him.

"I've secured bail for you, and just in time. Old Judge Smith was about to leave for the day. I've also found out what got you in here. Did you drive your truck back to the storage space last night?"

"Egads no," Cassia said. "No way I was going back. Besides, the headlights don't work or something like that."

Nate tilted his head at Cassia. "They rented you a truck without working headlights?"

Oh dear. That sounded pretty bad the way he said that.

"Can I get in trouble for that?" Just what Cassia needed. More trouble.

"Well, I'm pretty sure they can," Nate said. "I'm almost afraid to ask where you got this truck."

"Just some place down off 71. I can't remember the name."

"Is it some national brand I would know?" Nate asked.

Cassia shook her head slowly, apparently confirming Nate's fears.

"I thought not," he said. "Anyway, I'm trying to get a copy of the footage to show that it's not you, but in the still frames I saw, the glare of the headlights is obscuring whoever is in the driver's seat."

Staring at Nate, Cassia raised her eyebrows. Even after a dull day in jail, she caught the problem with that statement.

It took Nate a moment longer.

"The headlights that supposedly don't work on your truck," he finally said.

Cassia smiled for the first time that day.

The sun hung low above the horizon, sending golden light streaming on the front of Mandress Mansion, making even the old dark building in need of a serious paint job look warm and inviting.

Sheriff Andrews, Nate and Cassia, and Deputy Chester stood in the front turnabout where Cassia had parked the rental truck the day before. Normally it would have been a terrible spot to park, since it blocked other cars from pulling around the circle, but what was the point of owning property if you couldn't park any place you wanted to? When they'd driven up moments before, Cassia had turned in the passenger seat of Nate's car to see Sheriff Andrew's reaction when he pulled around the corner and saw the truck. She was amply rewarded by his twitching left eye.

Her parking job was his rule-of-order nightmare.

Why did that make her want to giggle? She was terrible sometimes.

"I think we have enough witnesses," Nate said. He took the

truck keys from Cassia and handed them over to Deputy Chester.

Suddenly fear gripped Cassia's heart. She had just taken the rental guy's word that the truck headlights didn't work. What if he was wrong, or she'd heard wrong, and now everyone would see them not only work, but now also have reason to think Cassia was a liar?

Cassia opened her mouth to say something about she had only been told about the lights by the rental guy when she caught Nate's disapproving look. Right. The less said the better. She shut her mouth.

Now if her dang heart would just stop pounding.

Deputy Chester awkwardly climbed up into the cab of the truck and turned the key to start the beast. It whined and complained several times before it came roaring to life.

The exhaust smelled awful, sending acidic and biting fumes into their faces. Cassia wouldn't have been surprised if the catalytic converter didn't work either.

Deputy Chester fumbled around the cab, looking at all the switches.

"Turn on the lights," called Sheriff Andrews.

"I'm trying," came the muffled response from the cab.

Cassia, Nate, and Sheriff Andrews stood in front of the truck.

No lights.

Peeling off from the group, Cassia walked around the back. The brake lights worked. The rear running lights worked. Deputy Chester was definitely doing *something* inside the truck.

Huffing, Sheriff Andrews pulled open the driver's door of the truck and motioned for Deputy Chester to get out so he could climb in. Then Sheriff Andrews fumbled around the cab, clicking switches repeatedly until he satisfied himself that the lights really didn't work. He turned off the motor and climbed back out.

"Okay, this isn't the same truck in the video, despite looking near identical," Sheriff Andrews said as he pushed his Mounty-style hat back. "That doesn't mean you're completely clear," he said to Cassia.

"Until you get more evidence, it kind of does mean that," Nate said to Sheriff Andrews. Cassia tried to look anywhere but at the two men glaring at each other.

By the time everyone left, the sun had set and Cassia went inside the mansion, putting off for yet another day dealing with any of the things inside the truck. Good thing she'd rented it for a week, although she was surprised her phone hadn't been blown up by David demanding to know when he and Kai were going to finish their moving job. He hadn't taken it well that first night when she'd told him she'd have to schedule the rest of the work later.

He probably wanted more fifties.

Cassia couldn't blame him on that. She wanted more fifties too.

"Meow!" Miss Mansfield called from her perch on the console table in the entryway. The cat glared balefully at Cassia. Miss Mansfield had been watching the goings-on in the front drive from the sitting room window and meowing at either the commotion, or else being left out of the commotion. The tiny white glint of her sharp teeth was visible as she cried, even from the spot where Cassia had stood on the driveway.

"I know, I know," Cassia said. "Dinnertime." Going down the hall to the kitchen, Cassia realized she was hungry too. Deputy Chester had tried to feed her but hadn't brought much except dry bagels and a bruised apple. Jail fare was not so tasty, that was for sure.

Cassia had just gotten Miss Mansfield's dinner settled when the front doorbell rang.

What now?

Trudging to the front door, Cassia peered through the peephole.

Genevieve stared back, only slightly leaning into the peephole. Cassia had to choke back a laugh. She knew that stance was taking all of Genevieve's willpower, because Genevieve loved to harass Cassia by sticking her face right to the little opening.

Throwing open the door, Cassia was even happier when the smell of steak meatballs and cheese bread washed over her. Genevieve was loaded down with a huge takeout bag from the diner and a six-pack of root beer.

"Heard you had a rough day," Genevieve said.

Cassia could have hugged her right then and there.

Inside the opened black metal dome of the telescope room constructed at the back of the house, Cassia and Genevieve lay on the wooden floor while wrapped in thick plaid wool blankets and looked up at the stars. The lights mounted on the walls holding up the giant metal dome were off, as were all the green shaded lights on the nearby worktables. The long barrel of the ancient telescope gleamed dimly in the starlight. A prized tool and centerpiece of the house.

What little warmth had been in the room had long ago floated up and out into the cold night through the open dome sections, but Cassia did not want to turn on a space heater or allow more heat to come in from the house through the door off the kitchen. If it did, it would just escape the dome in shimmering air waves, ruining their view and not benefiting either

Cassia or Genevieve in the slightest. No, it would have to be more clothes and blankets if she wanted to be warmer.

"Why do you like it so much out here?" Genevieve asked. It was as close to a complaint as she'd ever made about sitting in the cold observation room.

"Because it feels like family out here," Cassia said, the words coming out before she'd even really thought about them, but their truth was undeniable. "From what I remember of my family growing up, none of them liked astronomy. I always felt so strange and mismatched from them. When I was little, I'd actually thought the stork had made a mistake and had brought me to the wrong house."

Genevieve rolled her head to look at Cassia. "You're joking, right?"

"I wish," Cassia said. "I read a book about the stork when I was little and… well, I was sort of a literal kid."

Genevieve snorted but thankfully just went back to looking at the stars. Cassia knew she'd been a rather unconventional child. She didn't really want more confirmation of that right now.

"So anyway," Cassia continued, "when I came out here and realized there were other people in my family who liked astronomy, who *really* liked astronomy, I couldn't believe it. I just wish I'd been able to meet them."

"That would have been awesome for you. Perhaps you could have done your research out here," Genevieve said, glancing at the long tube of the old telescope.

"Not on that thing, even if it is really pretty. The technology they have is amazing now. They're talking about putting up another telescope in outer space with a gigantic sunshade to look for nearby planets," Cassia said, thinking back on some of the articles she'd read recently. "They'd stash it on rockets and unfold it like the James Webb telescope."

"Really? When do you have time to learn about all that

fancy astronomy stuff?" Genevieve asked, sitting up. She pulled the serving tray of meatballs closer to see if there was anything left. Just sauce. They'd both been really hungry.

"I don't, but it's way more fun than doing things like moving, or cleaning this place. I mean, I thought having a mansion could be cool, but right now it is starting to seem like a lot of work… and a lot of dead bodies." A dark look passed over Cassia's face.

"Ugh," Genevieve said. "We can talk about that tomorrow."

"Right. All the crappy stuff tomorrow. Except…" Cassia sat up.

Genevieve did too. "Except what?"

"I still didn't hear what happened to Owen Mensky. Do you know?"

"You mean at the storage space?"

Cassia nodded.

"Not really, no. I know that guy died during the night, and they think it has something to do with a moving truck. Apparently there aren't too many people at that place at night."

"How would they even know he died then?" Cassia asked, confused.

"Ah, I guess I do know something," Genevieve said, suddenly pleased. "Roger said the alarm company called in the sheriff."

"Roger?" Cassia asked.

"Yeah, because the sheriff called Roger next because he has the contract for maintenance for that place. Third call this week, and Andrews was getting pissed about all the false alarms."

"Except this wasn't a false alarm," Cassia said.

"No," Genevieve agreed.

"Huh." Cassia didn't know what to think about that. Maybe that storage place was not as nice as it seemed at first.

She lay back down to stare at the stars, distracted by the news.

After a few moments, Cassia turned her head to Genevieve, who was gathering the remains of their dinner. "What did David and Kai say about the move? Have they been by the diner?" Cassia asked. They better not have said anything bad about her after the horrid day she'd just had.

"Um, no. They haven't been by the diner. Trent was sort of wondering what was going on. David hasn't answered his phone all day. Trent said that was very unlike him. Plus, when Nate came by the diner for lunch he didn't say anything about anyone else coming in for questioning. Did you see anyone in the station?"

Cassia stared at Genevieve. What was going on?

"No, but the jail cell doesn't exactly give a clear view," Cassia said. Not that Cassia had heard anyone else speaking either. She'd been so wrapped up in feeling sorry for herself she hadn't even thought about who else might be a suspect. In hindsight, that seemed like a mistake.

CHAPTER 8

Cassia woke up early the next morning in her enormous bed in the first-floor bedroom of the mansion that she'd claimed as her own. The massive walnut four-poster bed and hotel-like nightstands equally reassured her and annoyed her at the same time with their plain and generic design. She guessed Sarah had picked the bedroom set out and that it was probably nothing like the room had been originally furnished by one of Cassia's actual relatives, like her Aunt Mildred, or her grandfather Senior Mandress.

At the foot of the bed, Miss Mansfield slept contentedly in a small circle of black fur. It must be early indeed for her to be awake before the cat.

Picking up her toy telescope from the nightstand, Cassia put it on her belly and thought about how different her life was than she thought it was going to be. If things had gone as planned, she would have been in Puerto Rico that very moment, doing exciting research at one of the largest telescopes in the world. Instead, the telescope had collapsed, along with her grad school funding, and Cassia had only avoided the streets by the grace of an aunt she hadn't even known existed until a few months ago.

How quickly things can change.

But she should be used to that, considering how quickly her life had changed after her parents had died when she was sixteen.

Seriously, could people stop dying around her? Especially the people in Forbidden Valley.

The terms of her aunt's will required that she live in the mansion for a year before she actually inherited it permanently, but judging by the way people kept falling like flies around her, that was looking less and less like a great deal.

Or even a good deal.

Oh well. She was in it now.

Cassia put the telescope back in its place on the nightstand and got out of bed. Shivering in an old UCLA T-shirt and sweats, she grabbed a sweater from a moving box before snagging her phone from the charger and heading out the door and down the hall to the kitchen.

Two cups of coffee and some mindless news scrawling later, Cassia felt ready to face the day. There had been nothing online that she could find about Owen's death at Mucho Junk. Maybe it was because it was too local of a story, or maybe it was because the police were keeping it quiet. Hopefully Nate had found out something about what had happened. As confident as Nate was about Cassia no longer being a suspect, she wouldn't feel better until they found whoever was responsible. Being the newest person in town seemed to make her an obvious target for suspicion, never mind that she was a small and innocent student.

"Meow," Miss Mansfield called from the floor, pulling Cassia from her internet phone surfing.

"Oh, we're up now? Did you have a rough day while I was gone yesterday?" Cassia asked Miss Mansfield. Did talking to her cat mean she was turning into a spinster old cat lady, or did you have to have a dozen animals before that definition kicked in?

Miss Mansfield didn't answer.

Cassia made quick work of opening a can of cat food and dishing it out, only to scream when she went to put it in Miss Mansfield's special area for eating.

Sitting right in the middle of the cat's dish from last night was that stupid brown mouse! It was eating the dried crumbly remains of Miss Mansfield's previous meal.

"Mouse! Mouse!" Cassia said, pointing to the creature and then looking at Miss Mansfield. Miss Mansfield just blinked her golden eyes at Cassia.

No no no! No mice! They got into things, and they smelled funny. Cassia had lived in a house with mice before and she never wanted to do that again.

"Get the mouse!" Cassia said as she nudged Miss Mansfield with her foot. The cat didn't move. Hyperventilating, Cassia dropped Miss Mansfield's dish of food on the center island and scrambled across the kitchen to the broom closet. Flinging the door open, Cassia grabbed the broom and pulled it out to swing at the mouse. She wasn't trying to kill the thing, just get it out of the house.

Considering all the doors and windows were closed, this was not going to end well. Realizing her error, Cassia ran to the back door and unlocked it. She flung it open to the weedy backyard.

Then, she ran back to where, unbelievably, the mouse was still eating on Miss Mansfield's dish and swung the broom at the mouse and dish. The dish came flying off the build-in desk where Miss Mansfield ate with the mouse riding it down like a surfboard.

The dish crashed on the tile floor and shattered. The mouse ran off.

Cassia gave chase with the broom, trying to corral the mouse out the door, but it ignored the open yard beyond and scrambled instead for the slightly open door of the pantry.

"No, no, no! Not in there!" Cassia yelled, but clearly the mouse was not taking orders from her for it disappeared into the pantry's shadows in a flash of brown.

"No!" Cassia said again, this time half-protest, half-sob. She just wanted one normal part of one normal day.

Miss Mansfield stared up at her, having not moved once during the entire chase. "Meow."

"I am not your friend right now. Don't talk to me," Cassia said as she placed the new dish of food for Miss Mansfield in its spot on the tiny desk. The cat blinked at her, then delicately picked her way around the broken dish on the kitchen floor to jump up and eat her breakfast.

Cassia sat down on the floor with a thump.

A long hot shower later, Cassia found some clean clothes and a nice warm jacket she'd forgotten about at the bottom of one last unchecked moving box. One of these days she was going to have to finish unpacking.

Unfortunately, she still hadn't gotten a better hat yet, so she was stuck with her green wool fake captain's hat.

Maybe that was appropriate. Today she was finally going to drive her own car.

Whee!

Grabbing her bag, Cassia took the envelope with the keys she'd gotten from Nate and opened the front door. She jumped when she saw the moving truck still out front. She'd forgotten about that. Well, that was just going to have to wait for another time. The mansion's contents didn't quite seem as important as they had been a few days ago.

After moving the truck off to one side, now resting half on the lawn, Cassia was finally ready to go.

She walked along the side of the mansion and under the carriage house to the path that led to the four-car garage off to the side, partially hidden in the woods. It wasn't the greatest spot for parking a car at night, but considering how isolated the house was, she had more to worry about from raccoons and coyotes than from carjackers or thieves.

Did coyotes attack people? Cassia had no idea. It was probably good that Miss Mansfield had no interest in going outside. Or knowing that cat, she'd probably get the coyote to do hunting for her.

Cassia snorted at her own stupid joke, the sound echoing unexpectedly loud in the quiet woods. Clouds fill the sky above, lending a softness to the landscape. Cassia's nerves twitched, until a gray squirrel ran by, followed by a much smaller but angrily chittering red one. Cassia's shoulders relaxed. Nothing too much could be amiss if the animals were out.

Her feet crunched through the dried leaves littering the gravel driveway back to the garage. Built in a completely modern style with a low roof and individual garage doors for four cars, it was probably best that the garage wasn't visible from the front of the mansion. It didn't look nearly regal enough.

Cassia unlocked the small door on the side of the building and entered. The car she was planning on driving stood closest to her—a white sedan with a black roof. It looked like the most stylish thing Cassia had ever seen.

Okay, maybe not the *most* stylish, but definitely the most stylish she'd ever gotten her hands on. She rubbed her hands together. Time to drive.

Grabbing the driver's door handle, which beeped welcome, she spared a glance for the other vehicles in the garage: a low sports car that looked slightly tacky and vaguely mid-life crisislike, another sedan, and what looked like a real Model T Ford. That was another thing to talk to Nate about. Cassia had no idea if those cars even ran, much less how to get the titles and insurance.

Perhaps this was a job for Roger. Did he do cars too?

Much to Cassia's relief, a plain garage door opener sat in the middle console of the car.

It only took about ten minutes for Cassia to figure out the controls of the car and get the garage door up, the chain creaking noisily but seeming to run okay. Another five minutes had her cruising past the mansion and down the road toward downtown Forgotten Valley.

Cassia grabbed the steering wheel and squealed. After a month of riding her bike back and forth, this felt like a magic carpet.

She glanced down at the speedometer and made another squeal, but not a happy one. Putting on the brakes a little too hard and sending herself forward toward the windshield, she brought the car down to the speed limit. With her luck, Sheriff Andrews would be patrolling just around the corner and ready to give her a ticket, or worse. He already seemed to think she was suspect number one for any bad things happening in Forgotten Valley.

The last thing she wanted was to spend one more minute in that dank excuse of a jail cell.

Happily, when Cassia made it downtown, she found a large open parking spot right in front of Nate's office. Her rusty parallel parking skills aside, parking was a breeze with the backup camera. The marvels of new technology.

She could get used to this lifestyle.

Exiting the vehicle, Cassia glanced down the street and saw a man in a business suit feeding a meter in front of his car.

Oh no! The meters. Cassia dug around in her bag, but after searching every pocket and corner, she only came up with a lot of crumbs, some blue lint, and one lone quarter. That was not nearly enough.

Maybe the meter took cards?

Checking the meter face, Cassia's heart fell. Of course they didn't. That would be just too modern for the antique shtick they had going on for the tourists.

One quarter it was. With any luck, Nate or Mrs. Anderson had a quarter or four she could buy off them.

"You think that's enough?" a familiar voice said behind her back.

Cassia slowly turned.

Sheriff Andrews. He looked the same as always. Cassia swore that man could be a robot. Clothes always perfectly pressed, his muscles bulging like he just worked out, even his blue eyes clear and never reddened with stress or exhaustion.

It was beyond annoying.

Purposefully, Cassia slowly walked to the meter and checked the fine print. "It is for twenty minutes," she said.

He crossed his arms.

What was he doing here anyhow?

"Don't you have a murder investigation to work on?" Cassia asked, a little snottiness creeping into her voice.

"Who says I'm not?" Sheriff Andrews said, his tone surprisingly matching hers.

Cassia stared at him while her mind leapt to several unhelpful and scary conclusions.

CHAPTER 9

Cassia realized her mouth was hanging open and shut it with a snap. Sheriff Andrews crossed his arms and then looked at Cassia's car and then pointed at the car fob in her hand.

Despite being a normal Friday morning in historical downtown Forgotten Valley, suddenly a chill went down Cassia's back.

"New car?" Sheriff Andrews asked, his voice dangerously low.

Was that a question she should wait for Nate to be around for?

Even as she thought yes, her mouth answered for her. "No. I guess it's new to me, but it's part of the mansion. I got the car with the inheritance deal thingie," Cassia said, starting to sound more incoherent by the minute.

"Probationary inheritance," Sheriff Andrews pointed out.

Cassia narrowed her eyes at him. Why did he have to point that out?

"I guess," she finally answered, not brave enough to just not respond.

Sheriff Andrews nodded like he had made some great

point and then turned and walked off, showing off that he must do squats as part of his workout routine.

Biting her lip to not make some stupid retort, Cassia crammed the quarter into the meter and then stomped into Forgotten Valley Lawyers, LTD.

"You sure you don't have any more?" Cassia asked, clutching a handful of quarters and standing in front of Mrs. Andersons's desk in the front lobby of the law office. As usual, the office itself was quiet, with sun streaming in through the large plate glass windows and no one sitting in the green leather studded chairs in the waiting room.

Mrs. Anderson looked up at Cassia and sniffed in disapproval. The older woman, sporting the largest bottle blond beehive hairdo Cassia had ever seen, was already miffed at Cassia for interrupting her typing. More than once, Cassia had wondered how there could be so much work to do on an old-fashioned typewriter in an office that always seemed empty.

Mrs. Anderson spread out the coins on the desk mat, looking for more quarters. "No, sorry, Ms. Lemon," Mrs. Anderson replied.

"I'll pay you for them," Cassia said, as if that promise would magically make more quarters appear in the pile below.

"I'm sure you will," Mrs. Anderson said as she picked up the mason jar perched on the edge of the desk and started sweeping loose nickels, dimes, and pennies into it, effectively dismissing Cassia.

"Okay, thanks," Cassia said. "I'll be right back."

Outside, Cassia shoved so many quarters into the meter it finally squeaked and refused to move, with one quarter still hanging out. Checking the meter face again, she realized she'd put in enough for four hours and now the thing wasn't going to budge another inch.

Well, with any luck that should keep Sheriff Andrews off her back.

For now.

The dim coolness of Nate's inner office worked its usual magic on Cassia's nerves. Swinging her legs, she sat in one of the large chairs in front of the absolutely enormous desk that was Nate's workspace. It looked normal-sized when he was behind it, but ridiculous when he was not.

"Feeling better?" Nate asked from the doorway. He entered, carrying two coffees in old-fashioned china cups on saucers and set one in front of Cassia. She raised her eyebrows at the painted delicate pink roses and twining greenery.

"Mrs. Anderson thought the new service would make the office classier," Nate said.

Cassia nodded. Of course she did. Classier, or just down-right classic, as in antique. Cassia hid her smile behind the cup. At least the coffee was delicious. Not that her nerves needed any more caffeine.

Nate settled himself behind the desk. "Did you sleep well last night?" he asked.

Cassia shook her head.

"I thought not. Pretty exciting day yesterday."

"If you mean exciting as in no-good, awful day, then yes, you're right," Cassia said. She took a sip and then put her cup down in its saucer.

"Yes, I agree. Awful can describe much of it. At least you didn't have to spend the night in the jail."

A shudder passed through Cassia. No, thanks.

"Did you find out more about what happened to Mr. Owen

Mensky?" Even though the poor man was dead, she couldn't quite help saying his name slightly sarcastically at the 'Mr.' part. He'd really been so obnoxious. "Who's investigating it? Because you know it seemed weird that Sheriff Andrews and Deputy Chester were in their office most of the day and not at the crime scene, if there was a crime scene—"

"Whoa," Nate said, holding his hand up. "One thing at a time. Did you make a list of questions for me, or was that spontaneous?"

"A list," Cassia admitted with a blush, "although I maybe should have added 'Wait for answers to the list.'"

"Or take a breath."

"Har har," Cassia said. Something about being on the hook for murder really didn't do much for her sense of humor, she had to admit.

"Okay, got it," Nate said in his best attempt at a calming voice. "As a matter of fact, I did find out some stuff last night after I left the mansion. One of my contacts in the cities let me know that a coroner got called on a job up here. I'm guessing that's the case at Mucho Junk."

"Is that bad?" Cassia asked.

"It means that someone up here is either on vacation, or else feels out of their element."

Cassia wasn't sure what that meant.

"Sorry, I don't know more. I'm usually more of a real estate, jack-of-all-trades lawyer."

"I know," Cassia said. "I wasn't trying to make you feel bad."

"Much appreciated." He smiled at her. "Now, I told you not to go back to the storage space, but that didn't mean I couldn't do so."

"You didn't?" Cassia asked breathlessly, hoping he had.

"I did. The sheriff's office was so tight-lipped, I thought I'd go to the source."

He finished and then just smiled at her from across the desk, enjoying the dramatic pause.

It only took one minute before Cassia couldn't take it anymore. "Well?" she asked impatiently.

"I found an older woman there loading stuff into her car. She said she'd heard a rumor someone found a body pinned under a garage door. That must have been Owen Mensky."

"How would she have known?" Cassia asked, confused. If other people had seen something and maybe been there when it had happened, why had Sheriff Andrews gone after her? Was it really just the video of the truck speeding away?

"She said some guy told her. Didn't have a description beyond he had blond hair."

That could be a lot of people. Talk about unhelpful help.

"There was still police crime tape up," Nate said, continuing. "Wasn't your space 2010?"

Cassia nodded. "Yes, one of the big ones."

"Apparently this happened at space 2014. The one right next to yours."

Ewww.

"That's not good."

"No," Nate agreed. "Better, though, than in your space. Another reason to have a good lock on it, I guess." He paused as if considering whether to share the next thing or not. Finally, he spoke. "The woman also said the dead guy had pieces of cigar stuffed in each ear."

Wow. Whoever did that really hated Mr. Owen Mensky and his cigars, Cassia thought, amazed and sickened at the same time.

"Cigar in his ears?" Genevieve said, making a horrified face.

"Shh! I'm probably not supposed to tell you," Cassia said,

holding a finger up to her mouth. She looked around the diner. It was quiet for a Friday afternoon, with only an elderly couple in one booth by the windows. Probably the calm before the storm that was Friday Fish Fry.

"What are you going to do?" Genevieve asked, round-eyed. She'd grabbed a pile of napkins and silverware and brought it over to Cassia so they could roll bundles together. Cassia wasn't an employee anymore, but this she didn't mind helping with. This way they could talk.

"I don't know. I'm not supposed to do anything," Cassia said. "Maybe they think I'm going to sit around and wait for them to solve it." She sullenly put a finished napkin bundle on the done pile.

"They might," Genevieve said, trying to sound hopeful.

"Like last time?"

Genevieve nodded acknowledgment at that. The last time Cassia had been suspected of murder, it had taken Cassia's investigating to clear her own name. Waiting for the sheriff to do it might be a dangerous game.

"Roger doesn't happen to do any work out at the storage space place, does he?" Cassia asked.

"I don't know. I can ask him." Genevieve took a large stack of finished silverware rolls and stashed them in the hostess area by the cash register. She came back with another tray of silverware. "Besides Roger, do you have any plans for investigating?"

Cassia shook her head glumly. The timing on all this was terrible too. She was just getting her stuff together to get the furnishings back in the house and maybe get some money or even just information out of the New York law firm her aunt had had some connections with.

"Has Trent heard back from David or Kai yet?" Cassia would have asked the man herself, but he was buried with work in the kitchen getting the fish ready for tonight. They were short-staffed in the kitchen that night.

"I don't think so. Have you tried calling?" Genevieve asked.

For an answer, Cassia pulled out her phone and showed Genevieve the phone log of calling David five times that day. Not a single pickup or call back. She would have tried Kai too, but never got his number, and of course he wasn't in the phone book since both of the men had both just recently moved into town.

Come to think of it, she didn't even know what town they lived in. She'd assumed Forgotten Valley, but that wasn't a given. Small towns filled the whole northern part of the state, interconnected with small two-lane roads. They could be just about anywhere reasonably close to downtown Forgotten Valley.

Putting her head in her hands, Cassia groaned. She really should be more careful about who she hired in the future.

"Did you tell Sheriff Andrews about David and Kai?" Genevieve asked.

"I told him everything," Cassia said as she looked up. "I told him about you and I visiting the space on Monday."

Genevieve winced.

"Sorry. I felt like I had to. And really, at first, it seemed like no big deal until they arrested me."

"That's sort of a big deal," Genevieve pointed out.

Cassia agreed.

Several hours later, Cassia squeezed into the small half-width booth tucked in the corner by the windows to sit across from Roger. Sound filled the diner and bounced off the walls as every seat was taken, and a few people stood by the counter while waiting for a spot to open. Even with fewer tourists from the cities, Trent had no problem filling Smith's Diner and Deli on Friday nights. Everyone loved all-you-can-eat deep-fried fish.

Cassia recognized a few people in the diner. Some, like Mrs. Jenson and her ever-present knitting needles, were regulars. Others, like the Smiths, were notable for both being regulars and also not liking Cassia all that much. They still hadn't forgiven her for ruining their plans of touring the mansion before the new owner came in and then having a gigantic party afterwards, even after she invited them to a party of her own. She gave them an extra big smile and waved from the booth. She was going to win them over one of these days, or just outright kill them with kindness trying.

She turned back to Roger. "Thanks for coming and having dinner with me tonight."

He rubbed his hands expectantly. "Thank you for the invite. You know how to win my heart."

Cassia had lucked out. She wanted to talk to Roger and he loved all things fish. It had only taken a text message for him to agree to let her pick him up and bring him for a free fish dinner.

Genevieve waved at them from across the room. Their dinner wouldn't be long now.

"So what was it you wanted to talk to me about so urgently?" Roger asked.

"You wouldn't happen to know anything about Mucho Junk Storage off Highway 71?" Cassia asked. She could have texted this question, but asking in person gave the opportunity to ask more follow-up questions. As one of the most skilled handymen in the north, Roger knew a surprising number of people and things. He was also highly bribable with the right food.

"Mucho Junk? Let me think. Yeah, that used to be called something else."

"Any name would be better than that," Cassia said with a small laugh.

"I used to know them as the prior company, but the new folks came in and fired me. That little guy... what was his name..."

"Owen?" Cassia supplied helpfully.

"Yeah, that was it. He hated me. I could never figure out why," Roger said. He leaned in conspiratorially. "Then, when I learned what he was up to, I didn't care why. I just wanted out of there."

"What he was up to?" Cassia asked. "Owen?"

"That guy was bad badddd news."

Cassia had never heard Roger bad-mouth anyone, at least not like that. What *had* this guy Owen been up to?

CHAPTER 10

The noise in the diner pressed in on Cassia as a loud group in the back cheered and then sang happy birthday to one of their group at a round table crowded in with people. Not only was Fish Fry night popular in general, it was also somewhat of a tradition to celebrate birthdays that night, adding to the chaos.

Cassia opened her mouth to ask about Owen when Genevieve swooped in with two large baskets of fried fish, fries, coleslaw, and homemade rolls. "I'll get your drinks in a minute," Genevieve said with a wink and was gone again before they could even thank her.

Roger eyed his basket appreciatively as he opened his napkin and tucked it into his shirt. He'd already tied back his wild white hair in anticipation of dinner.

Rather than try to compete with his dinner for Roger's attention, Cassia reached over for a bottle of ketchup and poured it all over her fries. Then came the tartar sauce. Before she'd even gotten a mouthful down, Roger had finished half his fish. He started to raise his hand to get Genevieve's attention for round two, but she beat him to it—arriving with two mugs of hot cider in one hand and a fresh basket of fish in the other, which she slid in front of Roger.

"Do I know you or what?" Genevieve asked Roger. He gave her a thumbs-up and then went back to his dinner.

Watching those two was like watching the inside of a well-oiled machine.

After twenty-some minutes of silent eating, Roger finally pushed away his third basket of fish. For a thin man, he ate an impressive amount, and quickly too. Cassia contentedly pushed away her own basket. Her first and last one of the night.

"That was phenomenal. Thank you," Roger said. He pulled a wrapped toothpick from the breast pocket of his shirt. He offered it to Cassia, but she waved it away.

"You're welcome." She smiled. "Now can I bug you with some questions?" Hopefully all that delicious food had put Roger in a good and talkable mood.

"Absolutely," Roger said.

"Okay." Cassia tapped her index finger on her bottom lip, trying to think of a good first question. "What was the deal with Owen? It sounds like you didn't like him much."

"Ack," Roger said with a look of distaste. "I liked him fine until I saw him giving access to other people's storage spaces for bribes."

He what?

Cassia sat up straight in the booth, suddenly tense all over.

"Isn't that, I dunno, illegal?" she asked, her voice going up in pitch and volume to end in a surprisingly loud squawk. Roger raised his eyebrows. A few other patrons looked over at Cassia. She cleared her throat and leaned in, bringing her volume down. "I mean, people put their own locks on the doors and stuff."

Roger just stared at her. Cassia turned beet red. She had personally witnessed both Roger and Genevieve pick locks and open things they weren't supposed to, and it hadn't even taken very long.

Dammit.

This is not a part of reality Cassia liked very much. People were supposed to respect locks.

But what really gripped her heart in a tight vise of fear was the thought of losing once again any possible connection to her aunt. It might be in one of the storage spaces of stuff in Mucho Junk.

If that sleaze Owen Mensky hadn't already dug around and taken it, or let someone else do so.

"Did you report him?" Cassia finally asked.

Roger nodded. "Much good as that did. I heard he didn't stop doing it. He just stopped doing it around me. Easy to do once he fired my butt."

That wretched jerk! Cassia thought. She'd never murder someone, but she was starting to understand how quite a few people might have wanted to kill Mr. Owen Mensky.

Unfortunately, that made things even harder for her to find the real culprit. There were possibly hundreds of storage spaces in that complex. Which meant possibly hundreds of murder suspects. Cassia groaned and slid down the booth again.

"Everything okay?" Genevieve said, knocking on the table to get Cassia's attention.

Dejected, Cassia slowly looked up. "Yes."

"Um, that doesn't seem very okay," Genevieve said. She glanced over at Roger, who just shrugged. Collecting the empty fish baskets, she lingered for a moment as if she was going to say something else.

Just then, a huge blaring air horn sounded outside on Main Street. Cassia had never heard anyone honk a regular horn in Forbidden Valley, much less use an air horn. She whipped her head to the large window and then scooted closer to it to look out into the dimming evening.

Outside, a few cars drove sedately down the main street, just enough going each way to clog up the little space left between the parked cars along the curb. At the far end of the block, a moving truck was trying to squeeze by a car where there was little room for another vehicle. It was only meant to be one lane each way, with no passing.

What was going on?

The truck revved up behind the little old lady driving a long 70s style sedan. The air horn sounded again.

The driver of the truck held the thing out his window. It looked like a gigantic can of hairspray with a big red nozzle.

Cassia squinted to see that far away. Between the distance and her refusal to admit she might need glasses sometimes, the driver only looked like a blur with dark hair.

Finally, the frazzled lady pulled over her large car partway into a spot much too small for it. The truck squealed its tires to accelerate around the protruding vehicle before traffic coming the other way could block it in.

Going by in a stench of smoky tires and another blast of the air horn for good measure, David Clyders barreled the truck down Main Street, with Kai Huntington hanging onto the strap over the passenger side door for dear life.

Cassia burst out the door of the diner, startling several patrons waiting outside. They scrambled out of her way as she ran down the street, trying to get a look at the license plate number of the truck now speeding away along Main Street.

The moving truck that looked just like hers, right down to the size of the box and the crappy logo on the side.

Except this one had working headlights. She knew, because

when it skidded into a left turn, cutting off traffic from the other direction, she could see the swing of the yellow lights hit the car coming from the other way and then lighting up the window display of backpacks and back to school clothes on the far storefront.

The truck disappeared from view, the occasional squeal from its tires ringing out in the night as it kept going.

"What the heck was that all about?" Cassia said as she slowed to a stop. The guy who couldn't return her call drove through town like he was announcing himself and then disappeared again.

Turning around, Cassia locked eyes with Genevieve, who'd followed her out of the diner along with Roger.

"Who drives like that through a crowded downtown?" Cassia asked before spooning a huge piece of lime pie into her mouth. Genevieve promised it would calm her down. Cassia didn't believe a word of that, but she was not going to turn down homemade pie.

Genevieve elbowed Cassia. She had squeezed into the booth next to Cassia for a moment to talk. "Slow down. You're going to make yourself sick."

"Am not," Cassia said with a mouthful of pie before swallowing. "You don't tell him to slow down," Cassia said, pointing at Roger with her spoon. He had his own piece of pie just because.

"I don't have to," Genevieve said.

Cassia narrowed her eyes at Genevieve. The first time she'd heard Genevieve's "older sister" voice, she'd been impressed. Now it just made her want to rebel.

"Anyway," Cassia said, turning her attention back to her dessert. She scraped at the last of the green fluffy whipped goo on the plate. "Something is up with that guy. At the very least he should be answering his phone. Plus, he has a truck just like in the video Sheriff Andrews was so worked up about."

Cassia's spoon scraped along the dish with a nails-on-chalkboard sound. Genevieve winced, then tried to take the plate from Cassia. Cassia held on, her knuckles going white as she gripped it and kept scraping off filling and whipped cream.

"Gimme," Genevieve said under her breath.

"No," Cassia hissed back. "AND," she said more loudly, "a man matching Kai's description was supposedly gossiping about seeing the body." Finally satisfied, Cassia popped the spoon with the last of the pie into her mouth and simultaneously let go of the plate.

Unprepared, Genevieve lost her balance and went flying backward to plop on the floor on her butt, all while still holding onto the pie plate. She glared at Cassia but didn't say a word as she climbed to her feet.

"All good points," Genevieve said in a falsely pleasant voice, then leaned into Cassia and spoke under her breath. "I'm never giving you pie again."

"Yes you are," Cassia said, then smiled up at Genevieve sweetly.

Genevieve huffed and then walked away.

"She is so giving me pie again," Cassia said to Roger.

He didn't comment.

He still had pie on his plate. Cassia stared at it, distracted.

He pulled his plate closer.

The rolling hills of northern Minnesota rolled out ahead of Cassia's car headlights under the light of a half moon. Stars twinkled in the clear night above. Glancing up through the moon roof of her car, Cassia appreciated the view of the swath of stars above, for once not freezing cold while doing so.

She had dropped off Roger at home. He'd promised to call if he could remember anything about the storage place, but it wasn't looking hopeful since they'd remodeled since he'd worked there. And Genevieve had been too busy to talk much. The backup waitress, Bridget, had only been able to work a half shift since her daughter needed her to watch the grand-kids. Cassia had almost felt bad about not being a waitress anymore, but then thought back to how awful she'd been at it and realized it was just as well.

Just then, her car spoke, startling her out of her reverie.

"Text message from Genevieve. Shall I read it?"

Holy cowbells. This car was too fancy.

"Yes," Cassia said tentatively.

"Okay. Genevieve says 'We need a field trip to pick up more stuff, don't you think?'"

A field trip. Ohhhh. To where? The rental place maybe? Spying?

Yes, yes, Cassia did think they needed a field trip.

"Do you want to reply?" the car asked.

"Yes," Cassia said. "Tell her I said yes, we do."

She pushed the gas pedal, nudging the car faster. She had to get home and get changed.

It was disguise time.

CHAPTER 11

Moonlight streamed into the entryway of the Mandress Mansion through the high windows over the double door entryway. It gave the normally cool open space a steely blue edge to the shadows. All the interior lights were off.

Miss Mansfield sat to one side on a narrow wood console, her black fur blending into the shadows, leaving only her eyes showing. The cat watched Cassia standing in the pool of moonlight in the middle of the floor, checking her phone, the light from the device shining up and making Cassia's face the brightest thing in the place.

"Come on, answer," Cassia muttered to herself as she stared at the text thread with Genevieve.

No text came.

Cassia pushed the call button, letting the phone ring.

"Hello, Cassia?" Genevieve said on the other end, her voice muffled and rough.

"Hello. I'm ready to go," Cassia said.

"What?" came the confused reply.

"I thought we were going… supply hunting," Cassia said, stopping herself from saying 'spying.' She was trying to get better at this whole 'plausible deniability' thing that Genevieve seemed so naturally good at. Like not putting incriminating things in texts or phone calls.

Not that going to her own storage space was incriminating. Or at least, in a reasonable world, it wouldn't have been. Even if they were doing it in the middle of the night.

"The stores aren't open now," Genevieve said. The sound of covers being pushed back came over the phone. *"You didn't think I meant..,"* Genevieve continued before her voice trailed off in a yawn.

"You aren't sleeping, are you?" Cassia asked, both confused and shocked. Usually Genevieve was pushing her to do crazy things, and not the other way around.

"I was. Did you see that crowd tonight?" Genevieve asked.

"Yeah, I was eating there."

"Well, I was working there. And it was hard, even for me." Genevieve said.

Oh.

"I think there has been a misunderstanding," Cassia said.

Genevieve didn't respond. Cassia hoped she hadn't fallen asleep. Just as Cassia was about to hang up, Genevieve spoke. *"I'll come by for breakfast tomorrow. Cool?"*

"Cool," Cassia said. She hung up her cell phone, feeling suddenly disappointed and alone.

She'd been ready for adventuring, but that was not to be tonight.

"Meow," Miss Mansfield said, as if she'd been waiting for her opportunity to get Cassia's attention.

Cassia turned to face Miss Mansfield. The curve of the cat's back was barely visible in the moonlit entryway. Miss Mansfield blinked slowly, then leapt off the console and walked down the hallway toward the kitchen. She stopped, turned, and looked back at Cassia and waited.

"Oh, okay," Cassia said as she started off after the cat.

Satisfied, Miss Mansfield gave a soft chirp and resumed walking to the kitchen.

Under the bright lights that Cassia had flicked on, the kitchen shone in a brilliant merging of whites and stainless steel. Much as Cassia tended toward clutter, even she felt wrong letting the beautiful space become disheveled and so kept it clean, organized, and well cared for. The only place she left any food out at all was for Miss Mansfield.

Which up until recently had not been a problem.

Cassia stared at the cat's dish, her hands on her hips and feeling decidedly unhappy.

It was absolutely picked clean.

Cassia had just filled it an hour ago, and while Miss Mansfield had a great appetite for a tiny feline, she never, ever, ate *everything* off her plate.

Which meant something else was eating it.

Most likely something else furry, brown, and very, very annoying.

Cassia really did not like mice.

"Why is this still a problem?" Cassia asked. She turned to Miss Mansfield, who just stared back. "You are a cat. Cats eat mice. If you are not happy with the mouse eating your food, then eat the dang mouse!"

Miss Mansfield merely blinked.

Infuriating.

Cassia grabbed the dish and put it in the sink, blasting hot water on it, then shutting off the tap with a thump. Behind her, a scuffle got her attention.

The mouse was back on Miss Mansfield's desk, sniffing around where the dish had been, its little furry sides breathing so quickly it looked like a heart beating. Of all the nerve. Shouldn't it at least be pretending to be afraid of humans?

Grabbing a drying takeout tub from the counter, Cassia slowly walked toward the mouse, lifting each foot with exaggerated care so as to not make any noise. Seemingly oblivious, the mouse continued sniffing around the area on the desk where the dish had been, grabbing and nibbling on tiny crumbs.

Making it almost to the desk, Cassia lifted the tub, preparing to bring it down upside down over the mouse when the mouse squeaked loudly and bolted along the desk. It must have seen Cassia.

"Oh no you don't," Cassia said as she scrambled to catch up with the tiny thing.

Sensing its danger, the mouse picked up speed, running along the back wall, and then finally off the side of the desk completely, landing with a soft plop on the kitchen floor. It took off toward the pantry doors.

Skidding in her socks on the slick kitchen floor, Cassia scrambled to change direction and cut the mouse off before it reached the safety of the doors. Why hadn't she shut them tightly before?

Actually, she had, Cassia realized.

It didn't seem to matter to the mouse. It kept running for the doors.

Cassia had to cut it off.

Pushing to run faster, Cassia slipped to one knee, hitting the floor with a painful crash. She looked up just in time to see the mouse slip *under* the completely shut door, flattening down like a piece of paper, wriggling and pushing with its hind legs until it was through.

Gross and amazing all at the same time. Who knew mice could do that?

But most of all, it was infuriating. No way it was getting away again.

Getting to her feet again, Cassia raced to the pantry, yanked the door open, then crouched down and pulled things out of the bottom shelf and shoved them behind her. In minutes the entire contents of that part of the pantry lay jammed into a messy pile against the base of the kitchen island, including a now ripped bag of rice flour that was spilling everywhere in soft piles of white.

Cassia reached in. She thought she saw a hole in the darkness. Maybe it was her exhaustion, or her frustration with the mouse, but she actually stuck her finger inside the hole and pulled, trying to make the opening bigger so she could fit her hand inside.

Much to her surprise, the inner wall of the pantry gave and popped out toward her with a soft thud. Grabbing her phone, Cassia turned on the flashlight and shone it inside the pantry. The back wall had come loose and there was something behind it.

The once clean kitchen lay in shambles. Every item from the vast pantry was out and on some surface. Boxes of dry pasta covered the counter to the right of the sink, canned and bottled vegetables to the left. Stacks of canned cat food took up a good chunk of the floor space by the back door, with bags of chips and other dry goods in their own piles on the floor and island.

The only uncluttered space was the pantry cupboard itself. It had held an amazing amount of stuff. How could a closet-like place seem to hold more than what comfortably fit in the kitchen itself? As a scientist and math proficient person, Cassia felt almost personally affronted at how illogical and impossible that seemed.

But the impossibility of the unending amounts of junk in

the pantry was not her biggest concern at the moment. No, that was the tantalizing peek she'd seen of something behind the false wall in the pantry itself. The problem was, she had to take the shelves out to remove the false door, and they didn't want to budge.

Cassia leaned into the pantry, using her phone to examine the wood joints of where the shelving met the wall. She couldn't see any screws or nails. Instead, the shelving looked almost embedded in the wall, as if the shelving continued on past the inner wall of the pantry. A thin bead of white stuff lay at the boundary between the wall and the shelving. Glue, most likely.

The easiest way to take the shelving out would be to break it with an ax and remove the bits by hand.

Something about willfully taking an ax to her inherited house struck Cassia as wrong, even if she really wanted to get behind the hidden panel at the back of the pantry.

How had this even happened? Did someone intentionally shelve in the false back of the closet? Or had it been simply forgotten about, or unknown, when the pantry was installed, leading to the closing off of the space?

Crouching on her hands and knees, Cassia peered into the pantry. She shoved her fingers underneath the thin wood piece and tried to lift the false back wall to see underneath it. The shelves themselves prevented her from pulling it back any further than she already had.

It moved up a fraction of an inch. Cold air blew on her face and a strange smell came from deep within the pantry.

Could there be a large space back there? It seemed so.

Would there be bodies?

Cassia shook her head. Where had that awful thought come from? This was not a horror house, but a beloved place of her family.

Where one body had already been found hanging off the observatory dome's spire.

Suddenly chilled, Cassia pulled back out of the pantry and rubbed her arms vigorously.

This might be a problem for tomorrow, when the sun was shining and someone else was with her.

The doorbell rang repeatedly, pulling Cassia out of a dream of the rover showing her around Mars. Some people had dreams of showing up naked in high school when they were stressed. Cassia had dreams of nearly dying from an overly enthusiastic Mars Rover named Perseverance who liked to yank out her oxygen tube and then take off like an errant dog.

Really, it was time for her subconscious to come up with something new.

Cassia stifled a yawn, and then jerked when she realized how late it was. Sun streamed into her bedroom from her poorly shut window curtains. Miss Mansfield was nowhere to be seen, unusually absent from her spot at the foot of the bed.

"Dang it," Cassia said. She rolled out of bed and caught a reflection of herself in the mirror hung across the room. Her hair stood up on one side and lay smashed flat to her face on the other. For long straight hair with no body, the mornings seemed to be the only time it wanted to do something adventurous, and usually not adventurous in a good way. Combing it down with her fingers, she stared at the wrinkles on her black pants and T-shirt.

She'd fallen asleep in her clothes again.

To be fair, that had seemed safer last night, when possibilities of strange passageways and possible bodies were just a few rooms away in the rather destroyed kitchen. If she was fully dressed, she could bolt away to safety without looking like a cliche from a horror movie.

Ring. The doorbell went off again. Cassia gave up on her hair and left to go answer it.

Genevieve stood in the bright morning sunshine, holding two coffees in a paper coffee caddy and a white bag of wonderfulness. A bakery bag.

"Oh thank goodness," Cassia said as she grabbed one of the cups of coffee, pulled back the lid, and took a sip.

"Good morning to you too," Genevieve said with a laugh, pleased with Cassia's reaction despite her protestation. She motioned to the dew covered moving van sitting parked partially on the grass and partially on the turnaround. "Are you ever going to unload that thing, or is this going to turn into a junk yard, rental van style?"

The moving van.

Cassia nearly choked on the coffee. In all the chaos, she'd forgotten about that thing. She had to get that stuff in the house. To make matters even worse, that was only a fraction of the stuff in the storage place that she was now afraid to go back to again in case she got charged with something worse.

"Yeah, sure, I'll unload it," Cassia said, feeling like a complete liar right out of an eighties teen movie.

"Ha," Genevieve said before she walked into the mansion. Cassia watched from the entryway as Genevieve reached the kitchen and turned in.

"What the heck?!" came the screeching question from inside the kitchen.

Cassia exhaled, her shoulders slumping. Yup, the whole thing with the kitchen was not a dream.

CHAPTER 12

Genevieve stood in the kitchen, her mouth hanging down, still holding the bakery bag and the coffee caddy. She probably would have put those down, but there was no place for them. Pantry items filled every inch of countertop space and a good portion of the floor. Cat prints left a trail through the fine white rice flour powder. Even the sink had plastic bags in it, making it difficult to use it for normal things like dishes.

Genevieve turned slowly at Cassia's entrance to the kitchen, her blue hair framed perfectly in the light coming in through the back windows. Cassia couldn't help but notice Genevieve looked like a comic book superhero. All that was missing was the rays of light coming off Genevieve, denoting her specialness.

Once again, Cassia marveled at who you could meet in a small town. How could she have been so ignorant of that?

"What happened?" Genevieve asked as Cassia went to the counter and used one hand to stack some of the biscuit bags on top of each other, trying to make room for Genevieve to put down her things. The pile teetered, stilled, and didn't crash onto the floor.

Genevieve put down the bag and caddy where Cassia pointed. She looked around the room, and then tried to pick her way around to the pantry. Genevieve had been in the kitchen so much even she knew where most of the stuff had come from.

Heck, Genevieve had purchased some of it, or had helped run to get it at the store after Sarah was arrested. Cassia had not had that much money then, and no car.

"Meow," Miss Mansfield said, coming into the room after Cassia, her black tail curled into a question mark.

Where had the cat been?

"Did you catch our friend?" Cassia asked, putting a hand on her hip.

Miss Mansfield sat down and started washing her face, completely ignoring Cassia's question. Of course she didn't.

"What friend?" Genevieve asked.

"The mouse," Cassia said without even looking up.

"Oh, yeah. I forgot." Genevieve opened the pantry door. "Is that why this is like this? To get the mouse?"

"It was at first," Cassia said, sipping her coffee and refusing to get closer to the pantry, at least for the moment. "Then I discovered there is a false back to the pantry."

"A what?" Genevieve said, now fully interested. She looked inside, and then reached in to feel the false back. It didn't take her long to figure out that the installed shelving prevented her from pulling out the panel and seeing what was behind it.

"Why would they do this like this?" Genevieve asked, motioning to the pantry and then wiping cobwebs and dust from her hair and face from digging so far in the storage space.

"I dunno," Cassia said. "To keep people out. Because they didn't know about it. To hide the bodies."

Genevieve laughed, a wonderful sound in the bright sunshine of morning. The situation hadn't seemed so funny late last night.

"There are no bodies in there."

Cassia stared at Genevieve. "And you know because you spent a lot of time here?"

Genevieve walked around the island to grab her own coffee from the caddy. She took a sip and then looked back to the pantry. "Good point."

"Meow," Miss Mansfield said again.

Right. Breakfast time.

"Alright, alright. I'm on it," Cassia said. It took some shuffling of things to get enough room to put a dish down and open a can of cat food. Luckily the piles of canned cat food were easy to find. Once Miss Mansfield was satisfied, Cassia returned to her coffee and the problem at hand.

"So what do you think?" Cassia finally asked. "Shall we break the shelving to get behind it? See if we can pry the shelving from the wall. I really don't understand how all of that was installed."

"Hmm. You really want to get back there. You know you could just put out traps for the mouse."

That was true, Cassia knew, but there was something about finding secrets in the house.

It wasn't just any house. It was her family's house. A family she hadn't even known she'd had.

If there were secrets there, she wanted to know, and she wanted to know what they were.

"Right. I can see by the look on your face the mouse is not the point anymore," Genevieve said.

Cassia nodded.

Genevieve's feet wiggled as she lay on the floor of the kitchen, half in and half out of the pantry, laying underneath the bottom shelf like it was a car and she a mechanic. Cassia heard a few grunting sounds. She and Miss Mansfield sat on the floor and watched. Cassia sat cross-legged, nursing the last of her coffee, while Miss Mansfield was in her normal regal pose, with her tail wrapped around her front toes.

Genevieve had insisted that it was a one-person job, not that Cassia really wanted to lay on that floor and do whatever Genevieve was doing.

A few moments later, a popping sound came out of the closet, then the clattering of the lower wooden shelf flying up and hitting the shelf above it.

Cassia sat up straighter, trying to see in. "Are you alright?" she called.

From inside the pantry, Genevieve coughed. "Just fine. Things worked exactly how I thought they would."

"What things?" Cassia asked.

"The shelves," Genevieve said as she pushed out of the pantry, holding the now loose bottom shelf. She sat up and put the large board off to one side. "It was painted in, but had been designed to be removed. I think the one above it might be the same. Only the top shelves are installed permanently through the wall."

"Why would someone design it that way? Half permanent and half removable."

"Well, you thought it was all permanent. It sort of does give that impression. You can get behind the shelving, but whoever put it in didn't want you to know that." Genevieve dusted off her hands as she found her way to her feet.

Cassia had to admit that was clever. She really had thought it had been built in and had almost given up because the only way back there would have been to break the shelving. She tilted her head at Genevieve. "How long do you think it's been like that?"

"A while. I think there were two coats of paint in the pantry. I saw a light yellow and..." She picked up the board and looked at the edge. "...a green. I can't imagine people painting the insides of cupboards very often. Maybe every ten years. Every twenty maybe?"

That seemed reasonable. And who knows how long it had been that way before the first coat of paint had been placed on it. Surely not right after it had been installed.

That little spot could have been hidden away longer than she had been alive.

Genevieve, Cassia, and Miss Mansfield all sat together on the front stoop of the mansion taking a well-earned break. The sun was high enough to have the whole front lit up and the warmth reflected from the mansion face warmed Cassia's back. There were some advantages to a dark paint job, and heating up quickly in the sunshine was one of them.

Cassia licked her fingers, trying to get the last of the sugar glaze off from the almond bear claw Genevieve had brought for her. Genevieve had happily eaten the chocolate croissant.

"So what was this about last night? Where did you think I meant to go?" Genevieve asked.

Glancing around, Cassia made sure their cell phones were in the house. She'd read about phones being able to spy on people even when they were supposedly off. That was not cool. There was no time like the present to start being more careful about those sorts of things.

"I thought we'd go to the storage space."

"Do you have something in mind?" Genevieve asked.

"No, not particularly. It just seems rather weird to be held responsible for something when I don't even know what happened."

Genevieve nodded at that.

"Remember how when we went to Wild Horses Banquet

hall? Just looking at the place helped us understand what happened," Cassia said.

"True, but we also had Roger to help us get the tapes. Rather illegally, I might add."

"Shhh!" Cassia said, looking around. Genevieve followed Cassia's eyes and looked around too.

"Are you expecting someone?" Genevieve asked.

"No, but it seems dangerous to say stuff like that out loud."

Genevieve raised her eyebrows. "Good point. You are learning quickly, young Jedi."

"Young what?"

"Never mind," Genevieve said. Cassia was starting to hate that phrase. Why did she miss half of Genevieve's references? Fricking story of her life.

"Let's go there today," Cassia said with a blurt. "To the storage space."

Genevieve checked her watch. "I have to get to work soon. Besides, it's full daylight out. Wouldn't you rather explore the hole in your kitchen instead?"

Yes.

No.

"Uhm," Cassia said, stalling for time. "Honestly, I don't know. Yes, I want to know what's back there, but no one has arrested me for murder for that particular mystery. Yet. The storage space situation seems a bit more urgent. Besides, I'm still holding out hope Miss Mansfield finally does her job." Cassia looked past Genevieve to glare at her cat. Miss Mansfield ignored Cassia, instead looking out contentedly at the front lawn. Cassia gave up and leaned back. "Besides, if you came with me," Cassia said to Genevieve, "I know you'd sweet-talk whoever was hanging out at the storage into sharing some information. You're so good at that."

"I am good at that," Genevieve agreed. Her self-satisfied

smile was almost a smirk, but had enough genuine goodwill in it that Cassia forgave her for it.

"So, let's go," Cassia said. She bit her lip to keep from saying please like a little kid.

Genevieve stared at Cassia. "Okay. But only if we drive separately, so I can go straight to work."

Cassia thought about it. She'd rather not bring her car to the Mucho Junk now that Sheriff Andrews knew what she was driving, but the alternative was exploring a dark hole in her kitchen.

"Deal," Cassia said.

CHAPTER 13

Cassia followed Genevieve's blue Honda over the curves of the country road to Highway 71 and then to Mucho Junk storage facilities. She'd almost forgotten the keys to the four spaces the government had turned over to her and had spent a frantic twenty minutes that morning searching the mansion for where she might have left them after the chaotic move with David and Kai. She knew that every minute she wasted was a minute less with Genevieve at the storage space.

Cassia could be brave about some things, but visiting the scene of a murder wasn't exactly on that list. She really wanted Genevieve there, especially since David had still not called her back.

Which reminded her. It might be time to visit Trent to find out what he knew about this guy.

Finally, they reached the front gate of the chain-link fence, then ran around the long parking lot of the sprawling complex. It was swung wide open and jammed into the wet grass, the links glinting in the morning light. Despite the open gate, the place appeared deserted. The window to the center office section looked dark, although it was hard to tell for sure since there was a white shade pulled down behind the glass.

Remembering their last adventure, Cassia looked for security cameras. Then she also remembered the reason Sheriff Andrews had arrested her was footage from security cameras.

There were definitely cameras.

The question was, where?

Cassia scanned the front of the building as they slowed. She leaned into the steering wheel to get a better view high on the buildings. There they were. One on each corner of the main buildings, and another nestled lower by the center office, aimed directly at the entrance. There should be no way to get in or out of the place without someone seeing.

So why hadn't they caught whoever was responsible for knocking off Owen Mensky?

The yellow and black police tape was still up at space 2014. Luckily it didn't touch the door of space 2010 where Cassia's stuff was, nor block the driveway. They didn't have to be quite so bold as to cross that line.

A dark brownish black stain marred the concrete at the bottom of the garage door for space 2014. Genevieve and Cassia stared at it from behind the police tape.

"Ewww," Genevieve said.

"Poor Mr. Owen Mensky," Cassia said. Then she remembered all the awful things Roger said he'd done, like stealing from people. Plus, she'd personally seen him make that woman cry and then threatened her, sort of, along with threatening Genevieve, David and Kai.

Still.

Getting crushed by a garage door until you left a stain on concrete was, well, pretty awful.

"Come on," Genevieve said. "We've got to get going. There doesn't seem to be anyone to talk to so what do you want to do?"

Cassia did not want to move stuff into her car, though part of her felt like that might be the responsible thing to do.

"How about if we walk around the place?" Cassia asked.

Genevieve turned around, considering the layout. The parking lot only took up the front of the building. There was no road access around the place, so the only way to see the back of the buildings was to walk around them.

"Sure. Why not? We can check for cameras and see if there is anything out back."

They walked down the empty parking lot to the far end of the building with the large spaces, going away from the central office area. With any luck, there would not be windows out of the back of that area, not that Cassia thought anyone was in the office.

Had they even replaced the caretaker position now that Owen Mensky was permanently indisposed? Or disposed? Inwardly Cassia groaned at her own bad taste pun.

"Do we even know whose space that was?" Cassia asked. For sure, Sheriff Andrews wasn't going to tell them.

"No, I don't think so. I wonder if they even know yet. They'd have to check the records, and if Owen Mensky was in charge, I'm not sure how up-and-up those records would be based on what Roger told you," Genevieve said.

"True. Plus I think they changed management. If someone had had that space for a while, they might have signed on under old management," Cassia said.

"That wouldn't have stopped Mensky from barging in and demanding documentation, or worse."

Cassia silently agreed. He had no qualms about demanding anything from anyone. Not that she'd seen.

The green grass in front rapidly gave way to the scrub of

weeds and prickly plants sparsely growing in the rough dirt on the sides of the building. The concrete walk didn't extend to the side of the building, so Cassia and Genevieve had to walk through the dirt and greenery. Despite the building having been there for a few years, the ground on the side looked like the desolate scrub that comes up around new construction when the landscaping hadn't been put in yet.

Cassia carefully picked her way through the plants. She had one of her few pairs of nice jeans on, and light tennis shoes. She hadn't really thought through dressing for this sort of thing.

They passed around the corner to the backs of the building, and the area looked even worse. A scrubby sort of bush grew in splotches here and there on the ground until the land reached an anemic woods behind the place. The sounds of the cars on Highway 71 faded as they walked back and the buildings blocked the noise. Much of the area lay in the shade of the tall storage space complex.

Suddenly Cassia was really glad Genevieve was there. It had gone from sunny normal day to creepy in about ten seconds.

They picked their way through the back. Out of paranoia, Cassia kept glancing out over the field toward the back woods. There were not many trees there, but enough to hide something or someone, she thought cynically, though who might be scoping out a boring old storage place, she had no idea.

Luckily, there were no windows on the back of the buildings, so at least no one from inside the buildings could be spying on them.

On one of her frequent glances back to the trees, Cassia noticed piles of dirt in neat rows halfway across the field. "Oh cool, they have prairie dogs here."

Genevieve stopped walking and turned slowly to look at Cassia. "There are no prairie dogs in Minnesota."

A lump formed in Cassia's stomach, her pastry breakfast suddenly not so comfortable. She pointed to the dirt piles in the middle of the field.

Cassia and Genevieve stood looking down at the dirt piles in the middle of the field next to several deep holes. There were other piles scattered all over the field. It had been slow going to pick their way there, since one slip of a foot into one of the holes and one of them could have broken their ankle. Genevieve had pulled Cassia back just in the nick of time when they'd come across the first one.

"What a blooming mess," Genevieve said, surveying the damage to the already unattractive area.

"Wonder if Mensky knew about this?" Cassia said sarcastically. The guy would have flipped his wig if he had seen this damage to his precious storage space.

"Unless he's the one who did it," Genevieve said. Shocked, Cassia looked at Genevieve, trying to think of reasons he would do such a thing.

Burying his stolen goods? Something didn't add up. Then it hit her.

"They are empty holes," Cassia said. "It doesn't look like someone burying something."

Genevieve kicked at the loose dirt on the edge of one of the holes. It tumbled in easily. The thing had to be at least two feet down, and strangely narrow. Cassia couldn't even imagine how it was made, since it was far narrower than the space needed to get a shovel in and dig.

"If it was someone looking for something," Genevieve said. "These holes look like the holes they make when they are putting in the posts for the hockey rink in our park. I know because I had to keep my young brother from playing in them when we were younger."

"How do they make those holes?"

"Posthole diggers. The gas ones are pretty fast."

Cassia didn't know what that was.

"Like a gigantic screwdriver," Genevieve said, motioning a circular motion into the ground with her finger.

"That could work if you didn't care about damaging whatever you were looking for," Cassia said, trying to imagine what it would take for a person to make all those holes.

Genevieve gave a long, low whistle. "Good point. Whoever did this was not playing."

That seemed true.

And chaotic. Cassia could not see a pattern to the holes in the ground. In some places they were so close together the ground almost threatened to be a big soft mass of dirt. Other places just had a hole here and there.

"Should we go check out the woods?" Cassia asked.

Genevieve held up her hand as sunshade and peered towards the wood. "Sure."

Unfortunately, or perhaps fortunately, the woods didn't have anything usual in them that Cassia could see. Just dead leaves in thick piles on the ground. They didn't go far into the woods because of the lack of a path.

"Come on," Cassia said. "Let's finish checking out the rest of the building."

The holes thinned out toward the far side of the back of the building. None marred the back grounds on the side of the building that had the smaller spaces. Cassia and Genevieve took the outside staircase that allowed access to the second-floor doors and walked the entire length of the space on both floors.

They didn't see anything that stood out as unusual on either floor.

No dark stains on the concrete. No broken locks or doors. Not even any graffiti. If Cassia hadn't known someone had been killed here, she would have thought it one of the safest places she'd ever been.

They walked back along the front of the building complex to Cassia's space.

"You know what's weird?" Genevieve asked as they crossed the asphalt.

"What?"

"We are the only ones here. It's a Saturday. Do you think they had so few customers?"

Cassia hadn't thought of that. The ads she saw for storage space when she'd been looking in California before moving out east had always said 'only one spot left at this price.' She'd just assumed the whole place was full. Maybe Minnesota was different and people had less stuff

Cassia paused in front of a door and knocked, as if it would echo like a ripe melon if empty. The metal door only tinged under her knuckles. Of course it wasn't possible to tell if anyone's stuff was in the space. Cassia stared at Genevieve and shrugged at the lack of response from within the storage space.

Genevieve laughed. "What are you trying to do?"

Turning a light shade of red, Cassia just said, "Thought I might be able to see if it was full."

Snorting, Genevieve thankfully didn't ask any more questions as they made their way back to Cassia's large space.

Fumbling with the keys, Cassia finally found the right one and released the lock on the large garage door. She pushed it up. The door creaked on the metal rollers, sounding obnoxiously loud in the quiet morning.

"Oh cute, what is this?" Genevieve said, seeing the white teddy bear on the pile of stuff the woman had dropped out of her car.

"Some woman's stuff. Owen was reading her the riot act

for taking things out of her space when she was behind on the payments or something. He didn't care she was bawling of course." Cassia waved to the pile of goods. "All that came out of her car, I think. I figured if I ever saw her again, I'd give it back to her."

Genevieve raised her eyebrows.

Cassia quickly clarified. "That was before everything went down and made coming here seem like a bad idea. And yet, here we are." She looked around the space. Despite filling up a not tiny moving truck, it still looked as full as ever.

Depressing.

Genevieve squeezed the bear as if testing out its cuddliness, then stopped abruptly and stared down at it. "This thing is crinkly," Genevieve said, then held the bear out, trying to feel around its belly.

Crinkly? "What?" Cassia asked.

Genevieve squeezed the bear in a tight hug, demonstrating. "Come here and listen."

Cassia went closer. Genevieve gave another, tighter squeeze. A sound between paper crumpling and a tin can getting compressed came out through the fluffy fake fur.

"Something's inside it," Genevieve pronounced as she held the bear out again.

CHAPTER 14

Cassia came out of the shadows of the storage space and back to where Genevieve stood in the sunlight streaming in the open garage door of the storage space. The white bear in Genevieve's hands nearly glowed in the light. The only dirt on it had been the bits from the parking lot when it had fallen out of the woman's car and landed on the asphalt.

It was pristine.

Not at all what one would expect from a well-used and much loved teddy bear, now that Cassia thought about it.

Genevieve squeezed it again, now just playing and grinning like an idiot.

"Stop that. You might break it," Cassia said.

"Break what?" Genevieve looked up. She had a wicked look in her eye.

Good point. What was in that bear?

"Who did you get this from again?" Genevieve asked.

"I didn't get it from her, directly. Exactly." Cassia didn't know how to explain it any better.

"In other words, you found it on the ground and grabbed it."

Cassia put her hands on her hips. When put that way, it sounded terrible.

"I wasn't planning on keeping it," Cassia said, a whine definitely creeping into her voice.

"Let's open it up," Genevieve said. "Maybe it's something secret inside. People always stash stuff in the weirdest things. It's always in movies and stuff. Maybe what's making noise is the electronic thingies for a spy camera."

"That you are destroying by squishing it," Cassia retorted, happy to have something to get back at Genevieve with.

"Oh. Good point." Genevieve's distress lasted for exactly one second before she looked up again, undeterred in her quest for adventure. "So one more reason to know. Let's open it and see." She bent over the bear again to examine it more closely, the bear now partially hidden under Genevieve's blue hair. Muttered questions reached Cassia. "I wonder if one of the eyes is a camera. Do you know how to tell? I'm not really sure…"

"We can't ruin it. It belongs to someone else," Cassia said, hoping that was the end of it.

"How about if we don't ruin it?"

"And how would that go?" Cassia asked.

Genevieve held up a finger. "Wait here." Putting down the bear, Genevieve ran out of the space and to her car. Grabbing something out of the glove box, she came with a small pocketknife. She unfolded it and grabbed the bear.

"Wait!" Cassia said, running to grab the bear from Genevieve. "What part of using a knife is not destroying it?"

"Will you give me a chance? Do you not trust me at all?" Genevieve asked.

Cassia eyed the knife. This did not look like a trustworthy situation.

"I can take the stitches out and then resew it. I'm good at that. Sewing I mean."

Cassia wasn't convinced.

"How do you think I get all the clothes I wear? From the local dress shop?"

Ohhhh. That explained so many things. Cassia slowly handed back the bear, still not completely convinced she was doing the right thing.

Genevieve gave Cassia a lopsided smirk, then flipped the bear facedown. She gently parted the fur along the back of the toy and then picked delicately with the tip of the knife. A few minutes later, Genevieve pulled out little bits of cut thread. The fur of the stuffed animal seemed completely intact.

"Wow. You did that like nothing," Cassia said.

"That's what happens when you make a lot of mistakes at first and half to rip out most all of your seams." Genevieve said distractedly, still working on the bear. She gently pulled apart the fabric, then stuck her fingers inside and dug around. A few pieces of wool stuffing fell out. Cassia ran to grab them before they got lost on the dirty floor.

"Ah-ha!" Genevieve said triumphantly, holding out a crinkled piece of paper partially sheathed in what looked like thin metal. It shimmered and almost looked like copper, but not quite as red.

"What is that?" Cassia asked, coming close.

Putting down the bear on the nearby pile, Genevieve used both hands to tug off the metal wrapper from the paper. It wasn't glued or stapled on, just wrapped around it. "I don't know. Never seen anything like this." Genevieve held the metal up to the light and examined it, but finally shrugged and set it aside.

She grinned at Cassia like a fox in the henhouse and then focused on opening the paper. It was folded over several times and was much larger than Cassia expected.

Genevieve's face almost glowed with her huge grin. "I knew it!" she said.

"What? What?" Cassia asked as she tried to look over Genevieve's shoulders.

A rough, hand-drawn map with strange symbols filled the page.

"Treasure!" Genevieve said.

"No blooming way," Cassia said, still staring at the map Genevieve had set down on a desk Cassia had pulled the dust-cover off of. "You know you are going to be insufferable from now."

"Why are you so mad at me for being right?" Genevieve asked innocently. She was digging around in a bag she'd retrieved from her car and pulling out spools of thread, trying to match the color to the bear.

"I'm not mad. I'm just… surprised this was actually inside of that thing."

Cassia saw what Genevieve was doing. She stepped in front of Genevieve to get her attention. "Is it really right to sew it back up without its contents? I mean, the woman lost both of those things. It's sort of like stealing just the same."

Genevieve frowned. "First off, it's not stealing because she dropped it and, two… dang it, you've got a point there."

"At least wait before sewing it up again."

"Alright. But maybe we should stash it somewhere so you don't accidentally give it back to her like it is."

Cassia thought about the woman in tears, and the horrid way Owen had harassed her about payment. Would she ever dare come back again? Impossible to tell.

"Good idea," Cassia said. She looked around, then pulled out one of the desk drawers. Empty. Perfect. Cassia shoved the bear inside.

Walking to the pile by the door, Cassia checked for anything else that might be interesting. A curtain rod, towels, the broken remains of a hand mixer and some assorted clothes, most with tiny flowers on them. Nothing too special. Only the bear had really stood out, or even looked close to new.

She returned to the map on the desk. A compass in the right upper corner marked north, but other than that, it could have been anywhere. No address. No coordinates. Nothing but some trees, some Xs that could have been anything, all drawn pell-mell in smeared ink. It didn't look like anything was on the same scale, leaving the trees as big as the buildings.

"Where do you think this is?" Cassia asked.

Genevieve shrugged her shoulders. "I have no idea. The buildings don't look like the storage area."

Cassia leaned in and squinted at the map. "They don't look like anything. They almost don't look like buildings."

Genevieve pointed. "The triangle roofs give them away."

"Har har." Cassia stood up again and stretched. "Maybe someone thought the treasure was out back," she said in jest.

Genevieve met her eyes. "Actually, that might explain a lot."

Cassia stopped mid-stretch. It might.

"Wow," Cassia said as it sank in. She walked out of the storage space to sit at the curb of the parking lot and think. It felt good to get back into the sun after the dim chill of the dark and not temperature controlled storage space.

Genevieve came and sat next to her.

"Think about it. What a great place to bury treasure," Genevieve said.

"Right by the freeway?" Cassia pointed to Highway 71 right in front of them.

"No, behind the building. There's nothing but scrub and some old trees back there."

"And holes in the ground," Cassia said.

"Okay, so does that mean they didn't find anything, or they found something and are long gone? Another thing, why didn't they cover their tracks?" Genevieve tapped her lips as she considered the problem.

"Maybe they didn't care if they covered their butts," Cassia said, thinking of the arrogance of thieves and criminals.

"Or maybe they're dead," Genevieve said in her best horror movie voice, waving her fingers menacingly in front of Cassia's face.

Or dead.

Genevieve kept waving her fingers in front of Cassia's eyes.

"Stop that," Cassia said, waving Genevieve away. This was enough of a real-life horror story as it was. There were holes out back, a strange map, and a murdered caretaker.

Could those things really all be related?

"Are you sure you want to stay here by yourself?" Genevieve asked as Cassia stood with her by Genevieve's old Honda in front of the storage place. They'd been there another hour and still no one had shown up. So much for using Genevieve's social skills to wring information out of strangers.

Where was everyone?

"I'm not easily creeped out by things, but even I find this weird," Genevieve said, motioning to the completely empty parking lot. It made the open gate even weirder. Who had opened the gate? Or was it always open, and if so, why bother having a gate?

Cassia nodded, thinking. "I wanted to go through some more stuff in the space, but you've got a point." She gave a small shiver. "Will you come back with me to scope out more stuff?"

"How about Monday?"

Cassia knew it was too much to ask Genevieve to work the Sunday rush and then come help her that night but she still felt some disappointment. Monday was two whole days away, but it would have to do. She nodded.

"Cool. Hey, go grab the map and lock up. That way we can leave together and I don't have to worry about what happened after I left," Genevieve said with a smile. She pulled out her phone from the car dash. "If I leave here in ten, I'll still make it to work on time."

"Okay, wait there," Cassia called, already running to the space. She grabbed her keys and her bag and the map, folding the last roughly and shoving it in the inner hidden back pocket of her backpack. Two minutes later and she had the garage door down and the padlock set. "Coming!" she called to Genevieve.

Their cars sped out of the empty parking lot of Mucho Junk storage spaces.

What Cassia had not thought about, she realized as she drove home, was that she now had to go face a mansion with a strange, and possibly very large and very old, unexplored area hiding in the pantry space of the kitchen.

Alone.

Something she really did not want to do.

Perhaps she could stop by a store, buy dinner for herself and Miss Mansfield and not have to go into the kitchen at all.

They could just huddle up in her bedroom and eat takeout and cat food on paper plates.

Not a great long-term solution, but at this point she just wanted to get through the day. It was only noon but already felt like too much had happened.

Not that there would ever be a great time to explore a strange, dark passageway alone.

At least not for Cassia Lemon. She was all sorts of brave

when it came to school and math problems and exploring the great unknowns of the outer universe, but strange holes that reminded her of horror movies?

That was all sorts of no.

No no no.

Which meant Cassia had to take a different route home to hit the closest market for something to eat that didn't require cooking or plates or anything at all from the kitchen. She looked longingly at the large flat panel of the computer screen in the car's dashboard. If she had just bothered to read the manual, perhaps she could have just asked the car for directions. But she hadn't, and she wasn't exactly sure what stores were around there, so she did it the old-fashioned way and got off Highway 71 a few stops early at what looked like a bigger exit and hoped for the best.

Just as she turned on her signal to take the exit ramp, a moving van came barrelling over the hill behind her. Cassia watched in the review mirror, fascinated and horrified, as it raced down the road toward her, at least thirty miles over the speed limit, until it passed her in the left lane and then at the very last minute swooped in front of her and careened down the exit, hitting the rumble strips along the side of the road as it veered from side to side.

As it went flying by, Cassia just got a glimpse of Kai Huntington hanging on to the strap over the passenger side window.

"David Clyders!" Cassia exclaimed. She punched the gas to try to catch up with the truck.

CHAPTER 15

The moving truck glinted in the midday sun as it headed down the exit ramp to the stop sign at the bottom. The exit ramp met up with a large divided cross street at the bottom, with multiple lanes each way and a grass median between the two different directions. Only a few cars drove each way on the road.

Either deliberately, or just by luck, the moving truck slowed just enough at the stop sign to keep from tipping over when it turned right, and then merged between two cars. The rear car honked and slid over one lane, narrowly managing to avoid crashing into the truck.

Cassia gasped at the near collision. Despite wanting to roar after the truck, she let off the gas and hit the brakes, slowing dramatically more than the moving truck had. She'd *just* got this car. No way she was going to crash it chasing after Tweedle Dee and Tweedle Dum.

She made a right turn to follow the truck, with only the barest squeal of her tires. Cruising down the crossroad, the lack of traffic was on her side. The truck ahead towered over the few cars traveling the same way.

The road led past a few gas stations and convenience stores. Cassia muttered as an elderly lady in an old green Pontiac turned into the road right in front of her, cutting Cassia off. Either the lady's vision was going, or that was the most passive-aggressive driving Cassia had ever seen. Cassia gripped the steering wheel tight and switched lanes to pass the ancient pond green beast of a car, forcing herself to not look at the woman driving it.

Her focus needed to be completely set on the moving van.

The one that looked just like her rental.

The one the sheriff thought might have something to do with the murder.

Much to Cassia's frustration, the road led deeper into a residential area. The speed limit dropped down to a near crawl, something the moving truck seemed to have no problem ignoring.

"What are you doing, David?" Cassia said to herself. She hadn't actually seen the man, but it had to be him driving.

Suddenly, the brake lights on the moving van flared.

The van slowed so fast the nose of the van dipped, and then the van jerked forward again, making a sudden right turn into a convenience store parking lot.

It skidded into a parking spot in front of the glass windows of the store, the tires hitting the cement curb stops. The vehicle stilled.

Cassia exhaled.

Thank goodness she hadn't been tailgating the truck. She'd probably have rear-ended the thing.

As she slowly approached the parking lot of the convenience store, Cassia signaled her turn to go into the parking lot, but then at the last minute lost her nerve. She didn't want to scare them off. She kept going and took the next right turn after the convenience store and parked on a side street half a block away and shut off her engine.

What exactly was she trying to do? Well, for one, she wanted to know why he had not answered her phone. And two, it might help to know where he was in case he had anything to do with Owen's murder.

Did David and Kai even know what had happened?

Cassia wasn't sure. Trent said he hadn't been able to get a hold of David either. He'd thought it rather strange since David was obsessive about returning calls right away. The only contact he'd had from David was a note shoved in the handle of the front door of the diner Friday morning. David must have stopped by before they'd opened that day. It only said David would stop by later, but he hadn't.

He *had* skidded by in the truck down Main street. Was that what he meant when he said he would stop by later?

Cassia took in a deep breath. She wasn't going to learn anything by sitting in her car. She didn't know why she was so nervous to go talk to David. Maybe because he was so intense.

Or maybe because someone had died recently.

Again.

But to be practical, David might have had nothing to do with it. From what she'd seen of Owen Mensky, the real hard find would be someone who didn't hate the man.

Getting out of the car and pulling her jacket tight against the brisk air, Cassia pressed the key fob to lock her car, something that still thrilled her. She walked back to the convenience store, hoping she had not made the wrong choice by not following the truck into the parking lot and it had since gotten away.

She hadn't.

It still stood there in the same parking spot with its engine off.

Kai lolled outside in the sun, walking in circles in the parking lot and sipping an icy drink an unnatural color of bright blue through a huge red straw. It looked full of horrible toxic food color and sugar, and suddenly Cassia wanted one of her own very much.

David came out of the convenience store, carrying his drink, but his was a huge coffee. He spotted Cassia and shifted direction, making a beeline for her.

"Cassia Lemon, are you ready to move the rest of your stuff?" He stood expectantly in front of her as if it was business as usual.

Cassia stepped back. That was not at all what she'd been expecting.

Of course, she had no idea what she'd been expecting, but it hadn't been the third degree about more work. Apparently he knew nothing about Owen Mensky's death.

Either that, or he was a phenomenal actor.

"Well?" he asked. "We might have an opening tomorrow. Have you unloaded your truck yet?"

"Um, no," Cassia said, deciding to answer the last question first. "I've been trying to call you."

"I didn't know," he answered.

How could he not know? He stared at her. Cassia started to feel uncomfortable. She glanced around the parking lot, as much to break off eye contact with David as to see who else was around. There were only two cars there, and the bumper of a third showed around the corner. Probably only a few customers and the clerk inside.

"Please unload your truck, or tell us where we can do so," David said.

"Excuse me?" Cassia asked, not even trying to hide her surprise this time.

"I think I dropped my phone in your truck," he said, as if that was obvious.

Ohhhh. That explained so much.

"I don't know where you live. I haven't been able to talk to Trent, and we've been extremely busy," he said, motioning to

Kai, who had just noticed Cassia and flicked his head up at her to say hi.

Cassia returned Kai's greeting with a small wave, which he took as an invitation to come join the conversation.

"How's it hanging, beautiful lady?" Kai said. His surfer accent was stronger than it had been the last time Cassia had seen him.

"All good," Cassia said, not quite sure how to respond. She could barely communicate with regular people, much less speak California coast surfer dialect.

"So?" David prompted Cassia.

What had they been talking about?

"So…" Cassia trailed off, not quite sure what he was getting at.

"So, are you ready to move the rest of your stuff? Like I said, we can unload your truck to save you time." He smiled in what Cassia was sure was meant to be a reassuring and charming smile. It looked stiff and vaguely terrifying, as if he was imitating what he thought a smile was and had no idea how to do a real one.

She smiled back uneasily.

She opened her mouth to answer, and then shut it again as she realized she'd have to tell them where she lived in order for them to come over and help her unpack.

No thank you.

At least not just yet. Until they figured out how who killed Owen Mensky, she wasn't giving that information out to anyone. Hopefully David didn't realize she lived in what was practically a county landmark and probably marked as a special interest location on half the maps out there.

Why did she keep running into the *cons* of being well-off enough to be almost famous? She was starting to think it was a curse and not a benefit after all.

"I would really like my phone back," David said when Cassia didn't answer.

"Right," Cassia said. "That's understandable. How about I unpack that this weekend and then, um, call you? No, that won't work. How about this? If I find the phone, I'll bring it to the diner. You can get it from Trent."

"How will I know if you found it?"

"Can't you call Trent from another phone?" Cassia asked. She pointed to Kai. "Doesn't he have one?"

Kai grinned at her like he wasn't paying attention to their conversation at all.

"No," David said.

"No?" Cassia asked, unclear what he meant.

"No, Kai doesn't have a phone—"

"Phones tie you down, man," Kai said. So he had been paying attention after all.

"Um, okay," Cassia said, turning back to David. "There has to be a pay phone or something you use. What about where you are staying?"

David narrowed his eyes at Cassia.

She backed up a step. "Not that I'm asking where you're staying. I just thought there might be a phone there."

Just then, the door to the convenience store opened and a young man wearing huge white headphones came strolling out. He walked close enough to Cassia, David, and Kai that Cassia felt a surge of relief. She used the distraction to back up a few feet from David.

She kept backing up. She'd clearly lost control of this conversation, and instead of getting more information, it felt like she was getting grilled and trapped into a corner. It unnerved her.

"I'll get that unpacked, and then we can schedule the rest of the move," Cassia said, raising her voice to compensate for getting further away.

David and Kai stared at her. She glanced at the truck over their shoulders. It had an out-of-state license plate. Yellow and blue. It would be great to get a photo of that, but how?

She bent down, pretending to retie a loose shoelace to buy time. She needed a good excuse to take a photo of the truck. But what?

It's not like she could say, *"Let me take a picture of your truck and your license plate"* without them getting hugely suspicious. Or at least David. He had acted weird enough when she'd asked about a phone where he lived.

A bird flew down from a nearby tree and pecked at the remains of a smashed French fry in the parking lot behind Kai and David. Seeing it, Cassia leapt to her feet and pointed to the bird. "Look, a rare Finch Warbler Red Neck!" she yelled, acting excited and grabbing in her pocket for her phone. She fumbled with it, acting like she was trying to take a picture of it and mashing down the picture button.

Kai and David turned, trying to find what she was pointing to. Their motion startled the bird and it flew off with its prize of the soggy French fry, leaving in a flash of gray.

David turned back to Cassia. She pasted her best dejected face on and pretended to watch the bird fly away.

"Cool bird, dude," Kai said, still staring at the bird as it flapped away. "Happy lunching," he called after it.

David still stared at Cassia. She reluctantly met his eyes. "I love birding. Great hobby. Picked it up in California. Amazing creatures. Really." She tried to smile at him to stop her word vomit. Her smile probably looked as fake as the one he'd given her earlier.

"Right," David said, completely unimpressed with the wildlife. "You unpack, give my phone to Trent if you find it, and let us know about moving."

Cassia nodded and gave him the peppiest thumbs-up she could manage, then turned to walk back to her car. She'd gotten halfway there when she realized she hadn't asked if they knew anything about the death of Owen Mensky, or if they'd been the ones to go back to the space that night.

She turned to go back but could see from where she was standing that their moving truck was not in the convenience store parking lot anymore.

They were long gone.

CHAPTER 16

By the time Cassia pulled up the manor drive to Mandress Mansion, the sun was already halfway down to the horizon again, leaving the dark manor looking even dimmer in the thinning late fall light.

She grimaced when she passed the moving truck still awkwardly parked off the front circle on her way back to the garage. She definitely did not want to be dealing with that moving truck after dark. There was no way she could really move all the stuff out of it and into the manor, especially considering some of it was large furniture that would take two people, but she could at least move some of the boxes. And look for David's phone.

How could he have lost a phone in the moving truck? Was he making calls from inside the truck? He seemed so strangely sure that was where it was. And if he was so sure, why hadn't he worked harder to track her down through Trent?

Something was not adding up.

The sight of the manor also reminded her of the big hole in the back of the pantry, in one of her most favorite places in the manor—the kitchen. It was like having one of her safe spaces yanked away.

Genevieve better show up to help her deal with that this weekend. Cassia could wait until Monday for another run at Mucho Junk, but the kitchen was different. She had to sleep in the mansion!

Cassia parked in the garage and then grabbed the bags from the passenger seat. She'd managed to get chicken sandwiches and a big Greek salad for herself, but had not had much luck finding Miss Mansfield's dinner. She could not find the same brand of cat food in the tiny convenience store she'd found. The cans in the store hadn't looked at all appealing, but Cassia bought a few just in case, though knowing Miss Mansfield, she'd probably turn her nose up at it. Cassia sighed, resigned that she'd probably still have to make a run into the kitchen to grab cat food cans from the stack on the floor in the manor kitchen and then hightail it out again so they could both eat elsewhere.

Miss Mansfield better not give her a hard time about that too. If she wanted to eat, she was going to eat where Cassia put down the dish.

Cassia did have some limits.

Fine dust came wafting out of the moving truck, along with a faintly musty smell that Cassia had not noticed before as she rolled up the now unlocked back door. Despite warm sandwiches and an irritated cat waiting for her, Cassia decided to get looking in the truck over with. Or at least started.

An intimidating stack of items faced her, several layers deep, and interlocked in weird ways to get all the strange shapes in. Small boxes were jammed inside the shelving of an open bookshelf, a large antique carved elephant placed inside the seating area of an overstuffed chair, floor lamps crammed to one side, with boxes of various shapes stacked in front of them, strange blanket-wrapped items Cassia could not even recall placing in the truck shoved here and there.

There was no way she was going to completely search the truck. Or even make significant progress.

It made her tired just looking at it.

She put her hands on her hips. How could she even start to look for a phone?

Lifting the skirt of the overstuffed chair, Cassia peered along the floorboards into the truck. Perhaps it slipped under the furniture. She saw nothing but darkness. Grabbing her cell phone, she turned on the flashlight and looked again, trying to see as far back in the truck as she could. The wood and metal floor gleamed in the light, dotted with dust and black streaks from previous moves. No phone.

Cassia switched off the flashlight and stood. So much for the easy route.

Wait. What if she called David's phone?

Looking up David's number, Cassia called. It went straight to voice mail.

The battery on his phone must be dead. She hung up before leaving a message. She'd left enough of those already.

She held her phone and considered the problem. Then she remembered the photos she tried to take of David's truck. Did it really look that much like the one she'd rented?

Pulling up her photo app, Cassia found a series of images consisting most of heavily streaked images of the truck, David, and Kai. Most were not even recognizable, looking instead like abstract artwork, but one was clear enough for Cassia to see the license plate colors of the truck as well as only slightly blurry images of David and Kai. She couldn't read the state off the license plate, but perhaps Genevieve or Roger would recognize the design.

Or Nate, though she really didn't want to tell her lawyer what she'd been up to. Somehow that didn't seem like something he'd approve of.

Composing a text to Genevieve and Roger, Cassia asked if either one of them knew what state the license plate was from, or if they knew how to track things by license plate. She sent the text with the photo to both of them.

Knowing Roger, he'd have some fancy gizmo for reading images better.

Which reminded her. Maybe he would have a metal detector. If someone had buried something out behind Mucho Junk, a metal detector might pick it up.

She sent another text to Roger asking if he had a metal detector too.

Feeling like she'd actually accomplished a lot, Cassia shoved her phone into her back pocket and dusted her hands.

She stared at the overwhelming mess inside the truck.

Enough of that for one day. She grabbed the woven pull strap to shut the truck again, brought the door down with a slam, and put the padlock back on.

Dinnertime.

Miss Mansfield glared at Cassia from her spot high on top of one of the moving boxes still stacked in Cassia's bedroom.

Cassia sat on the bed, her spread of takeout food on the nearby nightstand. She'd given only enough thought to cleanliness to remove her toy telescope and stack of astronomy books from that nightstand and place them on the floor. She didn't want her precious books ruined with food oil.

"Oh, come on," Cassia said, staring up at the animal. "Eating your dinner in here wasn't so bad. And I even left the water running in the bathroom for you. It's like your own personal fountain."

Miss Mansfield kept staring. Not a single loving blink. Not a purr.

"I braved the kitchen for you because you wouldn't touch what I bought you," Cassia pointed out.

Nothing. How could a cat stare like that without her eyeballs drying up like little grapes?

Whatever the secret of that was, Miss Mansfield had it down. She decidedly did not like change.

Cassia could relate.

"You know this is your fault, right, Miss Mansfield?" Cassia asked. "If you had just kept that mouse out of the kitchen, I never would have dug into the pantry and all that."

Miss Mansfield finally responded by standing and then curling into a ball with her back to Cassia.

Fine.

Taking another bite of her chicken sandwich, now only lukewarm at best, Cassia looked away and decided she would ignore the cat back until she calmed down. Hopefully that wouldn't take too long. She had no idea how long cats could hold grudges.

This was one of her first weekends not working at the diner. Her life had gone from culture shock from moving to Minnesota, to too busy to think while working at the diner, to now a little boring, with the possible exception of yet another murder that she was somehow entangled with. She had no idea what to do with her evening that didn't involve exploring an only slightly creepy at night mansion.

Amazing how much difference a little sunlight makes. In daylight, the mansion was fine, if a little large and dusty. At night, no thanks. And winter in Minnesota meant a lot less light.

Cassia groaned.

Stewing in thoughts like that was not going to make for a pleasant evening.

Finishing her sandwich, she balled the greasy wrapper and popped it back in the takeout bag. She wished she'd ordered more than two of them. It had not been nearly enough.

She wiped her hands on a paper napkin and then shoved that into the bag too.

Her room really was a mess.

At least her books were still in there. Despite the house having an enormous library, Cassia had been reluctant to store any of her books in that room. First, if she did somehow not satisfy the conditions of the will, she'd lose the house after all. She didn't want to lose her books on top of it.

Second, it galled her sense of control to not have all her books together in one place. It wasn't just the books themselves, but the hours she'd spend studying them, and underlining them (in pencil, of course) and learning about a whole new world that she loved a heck of a lot more than the one she had to live in. They had shown Cassia that the time and matter of the universe was so vast that it made the whole of humanity's existence on Earth was as relatively small as a flash of dust in the blink of a person's eye, all of which made it easier for her to swallow the simple past wrongs by the foster care system, or not having the funds for the coolest sneakers that everyone else in her old high school could afford.

In the end none of it mattered. Or all of it mattered equally little. The universe was cool and amazing and she'd been lucky enough to exist in it and see just a fraction of what was out there.

She'd never been able to explain those thoughts to anyone else, but they had always calmed her.

She needed some of that calm now.

Grabbing a book called *Galactic Star Dynamics, or Why Spiral*

Galaxies Make the Best Neighbors off the floor, Cassia shuffled back to the headboard and settled in for a good read.

Perseverance poked at Cassia, its round camera eye blinking.

Cassia lay in an enormous NASA space suit on the dusty ground of Mars. Faint red dust covered the front mirrored surface of her helmet, giving everything a reddish tint.

She stared up at the stars. The daytime sky was only a slightly lighter shade of black. There was not enough atmosphere to make anything even close to the beautiful blue sky of Earth.

Where she should have been.

Cassia knew she was dreaming. She'd had enough of these dreams to know by now. Sometimes she tried to stay in them and see what happened. Despite knowing it not being real, sometimes it seemed like she learned something that helped in her real life.

Plus, it was fun spending time on Mars, something she'd likely not ever get to do in real life.

Perseverance poked her again, this time revving an engine in its shoulder, sounding faintly like a purr. It wanted Cassia to get up.

She tried to pet it on its head, but it rolled back, its six wheels throwing up a light layer of Martian dust that fell down in the slow-motion look of lighter gravity.

Suddenly, Perseverance swung its head to look behind itself. Something had its attention. Cassia lifted her head to see. In the distance it looked like a gigantic mouse ran behind a rock.

A mouse?

Never mind the impossibility of anything living there with no air.

Perseverance whipped off a three-point turn and then tore off across the red ground to where the mouse had disappeared.

Good Rover, Cassia thought. Teach that to my cat.

She watched the Rover chase after the mouse and then realized there were other mice hiding behind other rocks.

One in almost every direction she looked.

Cassia sat up, her heart now racing in her chest. A cold sweat broke out over her back and neck, making her feel ill and dizzy in what had been a comfortable suit.

One mouse ran across the ground, setting off a trail like a rocket-powered car behind it, and raced up to her. Before she could react to the golden-retriever-sized mouse, it reached out and nipped her on her space suit wrist with its gigantic white teeth, leaving a ragged hole.

CHAPTER 17

Even knowing it was a dream, Cassia still woke up in a terror. The sweat from her dream had been real enough, soaking her clothes and bedcover. Once again, she'd fallen asleep in her clothes, the heavy copy of her astronomy book open and lying pages down on her chest.

Her mouth tasted terrible. Failing to brush her teeth after chicken sandwiches and the onion-heavy Greek salad had been a mistake.

Miss Mansfield was nowhere to be seen. She could be anywhere in the huge mansion—all except for inside the pantry. Cassia had made sure of that, shutting the pantry doors firmly and pushing a few stacks of cans in front of it in case the cat somehow figured out how to pull the doors open.

The overhead light and bedside lamp both burned a warm yellow in the room. With the heavy curtains pulled shut across the window, Cassia had no idea what time it was.

Spying her phone on the bed a few feet away, Cassia grabbed it and sat up on her elbows to check the time. 6:50 am. Almost time to get up. Certainly not enough time to change into her pajamas and crawl back into bed, as much as she wanted to.

Her phone vibrated. Cassia nearly dropped it.

A text notification dropped down. It was from Genevieve.

"Want some help in the pantry?"

Did she ever.

Cassia blearily stared at the phone as she typed back "yes".

"Okay. I'll be there in twenty."

What? Twenty minutes? Cassia blinked, looking around at the chaotic mess of her bedroom, and frankly, herself.

Much as Cassia wanted to argue, she just texted back, *"great."*

Cassia Lemon did not look a gift horse in the mouth.

Genevieve brushed past Cassia to walk straight back to the kitchen. The sun had not yet risen, so Cassia had opened the door to Genevieve framed in a pretty orange and pink pre-sunrise sky.

Genevieve's hair and outfit looked perfect. Cassia had expected her normal pre-work plain black jeans, but Genevieve looked like she was ready to go out in public, with a linen white shirt underneath a black custom-made denim jacket with straps and patches, along with matching pants crisscrossed with straps. Now that Cassia knew Genevieve made her own clothes, she was even more impressed.

"You're wearing that to the diner?" Cassia asked.

"Not today. Bridget wanted my shift. She wants to surprise her daughter and grandkids with a trip to the Mall of America and needed the cash. Not my idea of fun, but hey, I got out of Sunday brunch."

That sounded great to Cassia. "And you're spending it with me?" Cassia asked, pleased and almost surprised.

"The thought of you tiptoeing around this mansion because there is a hole in your pantry pains me. Why are you so afraid of whatever is back there?"

"Because this place is twenty-six miles outside of town, which means any help is at least forty minutes away, and wildlife scares me."

"A mouse," Genevieve said as she turned into the kitchen and once again winced at the sight of the mess. If anything, it was worse because Cassia had accidentally knocked over a bottle of window cleaner in her rush to get cat food and had done a less than stellar job wiping it up. The kitchen still smelled faintly of vinegar.

"Are mice tame?"

"You are like twenty times its size. Or more."

"But it could get me while I'm sleeping, or have diseases."

"I know kindergarteners who are braver than you," Genevieve said as she helped herself to the drawer of coffee pods and grabbed a cup to make herself some. "Sorry, I didn't get to the bakery this am. I thought you'd forgive me."

"Forgive you? I'll buy you lunch, just as long as you don't make that kindergartener remark again."

Genevieve chuckled. "Deal."

Two cups of coffee and one fed cat later, Cassia felt ready to deal with the pantry. Genevieve caught her glance at it.

"Let's do this thing," Genevieve said. Cassia nodded.

Pushing away the stacks of cans, Genevieve opened the doors to the pantry as wide as she could, trying to get some light inside to see better. She'd already pulled out the bottom two shelves and loosened the back panel of the pantry. All that was left was to pull the panel out and see what was behind there.

Unfortunately that involved a lot of sitting and crawling on the non-too-clean interior of the old shelving.

Genevieve looked down at her nice clothes. "I don't think I thought this through."

Cassia had to laugh. She could have gone in there and no one probably would have noticed with what she was wearing. Not that she wanted to. "I've got something for you"

Genevieve looked up at her skeptically.

Genevieve did look cute in Cassia's UCLA blue and gold sweats. The blue in the sweatshirt almost matched the faded blue of Genevieve's once dark blue hair. The gold pants were a nice touch, with just a hint of high water from her taller height over Cassia.

Genevieve did not agree. She glowered at herself in the full-length mirror in Cassia's bedroom, then turned to look daggers at Cassia.

"No one will see," Cassia said. Unless she took a picture, which judging by Genevieve's reaction, she didn't dare. Not if she wanted help with the pantry or to keep her closest friend in this northern wilderness.

No, she'd have to treasure this memory in her mind instead.

"Fine. But you're washing this stuff when we're done. I am not bringing this home. I don't have a private laundry," Genevieve said. Cassia just nodded, afraid she'd giggle if she tried to say anything else.

Once back in the kitchen, Genevieve wasted no time going to the pantry and getting on her hand and knees to try to pull out the back panel of the space. It moved a little, but still didn't have enough room to slide forward from the bottom.

Genevieve wiggled and pulled on it, muttering and throwing up a cloud of dust in her struggles. Finally, she gave up and sat down on the floor, then pushed herself away from the pantry to look up and evaluate its geometry.

"Another layer of shelving has to come out," Genevieve finally said. "There's no other way."

Cassia squinted at the wide space. That next level of shelving looked permanent. Genevieve turned back to meet her gaze.

"It looks solid, doesn't it?" Genevieve said.

Cassia nodded.

"I'm betting it's not. Why bother to be so clever, but not do it right completely?" Genevieve asked, but she wasn't waiting for an answer from Cassia. She scooted forward and hit the shelving in question from below swiftly with the heel of her hand. The paint on either side cracked, like breaking the seal on a jar. "Thought so," Genevieve said as she hit the shelving again. This time it popped up, free from the walls on either side. Genevieve caught it and pulled it out of the pantry.

She stood and dusted herself off. "Okay, let's try again." Genevieve reached into the lower section of the back panel. This time she was able to slide it forward along the floor. The top of the back panel tipped back into what Cassia now realized was a huge void behind the pantry space.

All that time Cassia had lived here thinking it was a normal kitchen and there was a gaping space of who knows what back there.

It got worse when Genevieve pulled the large panel out completely and leaned it up against the side wall.

The entire space behind the pantry was open, from floor to ceiling. It looked wide enough for one person to walk through, but just barely that big. It was impossible to see what lay in the darkness beyond the back edge of the remaining shelves.

A shiver went down Cassia's spine.

No no no. She did not like haunted houses, horror movies, or this. All the nopes.

Genevieve rubbed her hands in excitement. She pretty much had the opposite response.

"Aren't you worried about what's back there?" Cassia asked.

Genevieve turned and winked at Cassia. "Not at all. What are you worried about? Unless this leads to a tunnel to the outside—which would be exciting," Genevieve nearly sang the word exciting, "anything left inside would be long dead."

"Great. Dead bodies," Cassia said.

"I'm sure there are no dead bodies in there," Genevieve said. "Besides, that would stink I'm sure. This smells just fine."

Cassia wasn't so sure about Genevieve's logic, but she did appreciate her sense of adventure. Normally, Cassia thought of herself as brave and adventurous. Clearly this was not true in all circumstances.

"Do you have any flashlights?" Genevieve asked.

Did she? There was one buried somewhere in one of her moving boxes, but Cassia couldn't remember which one. "How about we use our phones?" Cassia suggested.

Lighting up both their phones, Cassia and Genevieve stood in the doorway to the pantry and shone the lights in. The blackness *was* a tunnel leading back and curving out of sight.

What was behind that section of the kitchen? Cassia had thought it was the sitting room opposite to the library, but clearly there was something else between the two rooms. Was her spatial sense that far off that she never noticed that one of the rooms should have been bigger?

"Let's go," Genevieve said with a way too enthusiastic smile.

Against her better judgment, Cassia motioned for Genevieve to lead the way.

The passageway, though dark and damp, was surprisingly clean. Being sealed off from the rest of the house apparently kept a lot of the dust out. The floor was wooden, as were the walls. Only the entryway had the plaster walls of the rest of the house. This part felt like it was never meant to be seen by others, or at least not publicly.

Once the passageway turned a gentle left, it came upon a narrow set of stairs. Cassia thought if her shoulders had been any wider, they would have touched on both sides when going down, which was good, because there was no handrail on either side. This was all constructed long before any sort of public safety codes were put into place. Or maybe an inspector was never meant to see this part of the house at all.

After going down what seemed like more than a single flight of stairs, they reached a tiny room, maybe ten feet to a side, with a dirt floor. A flimsy wooden table that looked painted pink in the light of the flashlights rested behind the wooden staircase. The only thing on the table was an old-fashioned metal box, painted with a scene of a young man with rosy cheeks sitting next to a young woman in a garden and offering her flowers.

"Wow, look at that," Genevieve said, going to the tin. She touched one of the front corners and lifted it. It opened on a hinge, revealing the insides like a book opening up.

Cassia crowded around with Genevieve. The tin itself looked ancient. Inside, some folded linen enclosed whatever else was inside.

Genevieve gently lifted a corner of the linen, and when nothing immediately appeared, pulled it back and lifted the inner layer of material.

Inside, a stack of black-and-white photographs nestled.

"Oh my," Cassia said quietly. She reached past Genevieve and took the photos. There were a lot of them.

And below the photographs, three shiny gold coins lay.

Two of the coins had a woman in flowing robes walking toward the viewer, and the third a flying eagle. Genevieve stared at the coins and whistled low.

"1908. I bet those are real gold."

As precious as gold was, Cassia was more interested in the photos. The first had a young man in a rounded bowler hat in a large fancy public square that looked like nothing Cassia had ever seen in America. Next to him a woman in a twenties flapper outfit mugged for the camera. This picture had to have been taken a hundred years ago.

The next picture took Cassia's breath away. Posing next to a 1960 AMC Rambler in front of a cornfield stood a girl with straight dark hair, an ill-fitting dress, and wearing Cassia's face.

Genevieve peered over Cassia's shoulder. "Holy moly, girl, she looks exactly like you!"

CHAPTER 18

Cassia held the black-and-white photo in the dim basement area and felt like she was having an out-of-body experience. The woman in it really did look *just* like her.

It was almost creepy.

Genevieve peered closer to the photo, pushing in on Cassia's arm.

Suddenly the cool and quiet space felt far too closed in and crowded to Cassia. The dirt floor and tight walls around her made her think more of the walls of a casket and not of a basement in a huge mansion.

"Must get out," Cassia said, not even caring that she sounded a little erratic. She felt erratic.

To Genevieve's credit, she didn't have to be asked twice. Genevieve took the photos from Cassia's hands, shoved them back in the tin box, tucked the box under one arm, and grabbed Cassia with the other, all while still aiming her cell phone flashlight.

Genevieve pulled Cassia behind her as she went up the stairs and led Cassia back out the pantry tunnel into the kitchen. Nudging Cassia over to a stool in front of the kitchen island, Genevieve gingerly stepped over all the items on the floor to make her way to the refrigerator. After some digging in the vast stainless steel monstrosity, she reemerged with a cold root beer.

She poured the fizzing drink into a glass and set it in front of Cassia. "Drink."

Cassia just stared at the drink for a moment. She felt funny.

"Drink," Genevieve insisted.

Finally doing as she was told, Cassia drank the ice-cold root beer. The sugar hit her like a wave.

A few moments later she felt better.

"What was that all about?" Cassia asked as she finished the drink, the scientist in her wanting to know.

"I don't know exactly," Genevieve admitted. "I just know something sweet helps people deal with shocking things, and that picture was quite the shocker."

Cassia was going to have to remember that in the future. Hopefully she'd never need it.

Grabbing the tin box from the counter where she'd left it, Genevieve brought it over to the island. She opened it and pulled out the photos, handing them to Cassia.

"Does it say who it is?" Genevieve asked.

Confused, Cassia looked down at the top photograph that could have been her if she'd found a time machine and went back to the 1950s or so. Then she thought to flip it over. In a beautiful script it said *M Mandress*. M Mandress. Mildred Mandress? This was her aunt that she'd never met? And her father never thought Cassia should know about her when they looked like they could have been identical twins?

After a moment Cassia realized she might not be being entirely fair. Her aunt had been fairly old when Cassia's father had been born, and he'd died when Cassia was just sixteen.

Maybe he hadn't known.

Genevieve sprawled out on the front lawn in the sunshine, the once pristine gold sweatpants now streaked with dirt. A matching streak ran across her nose and across one cheek. The UCLA on her sweatshirt now just said CLA, with the U nearly obscured by dirt.

Cassia was sure she didn't look any better. She really hadn't started much better anyhow, having slept in her clothes. But now she probably looked worse. At least dirtier.

The contents of the moving truck lay all around the front drive, and scattered here and there on the grass. It reminded Cassia of those clown car skits. There was no way all that stuff had come out of the moving truck. And yet it had.

Now it had to go into the mansion somewhere.

Cassia flopped back on the grass. It wasn't all that warm out, but it felt good for now since the sun was out and she'd worked up a sweat pulling stuff out with Genevieve. David and Kai had loaded the thing up back at Mucho Junk, so she really hadn't appreciated how much they'd packed in there until she had to pull it out herself.

More and more, she was starting to think owning stuff was a curse. At least if you had to lug it around yourself.

"Okay, so no cell phone in any of the furniture and knick-knacks," Genevieve said, ticking off points on her hands. "So now we should check the boxes." She stared over at Cassia.

Cassia groaned.

"Why exactly did he think he left it in the truck?" Genevieve asked.

"I have no idea," Cassia said. "I think it's weird too."

"Do you think he was trying to intentionally find out where you live?" Genevieve asked.

Whoa, what?

"Excuse me?" Cassia said.

"You know, GPS tracking and all that."

Holy cannolis. Cassia had *not* thought of that.

"But the phone's dead. I'm pretty sure," Cassia said, grasping at anything to make herself feel better.

"Yeah, but it probably wasn't when you drove home that day," Genevieve said, pointing out something Cassia very much did not want to think about.

No no no. This was so not good.

"Maybe it wasn't intentional," Cassia said.

"Maybe," Genevieve said. She didn't sound too hopeful.

Cassia scrambled to her feet. She couldn't do anything about it now, but she really wanted to find that phone, so maybe she could stomp on it or something. It might not fix anything, but it sounded like something she really wanted to do.

More stuff littered the area in front of the mansion, this time in the forms of papers. Despite Cassia and Genevieve's best efforts, it was nearly impossible to put things back in the boxes the way they had taken them out. Perhaps it was their lack of patience in that they were now racing the sun, or just exhaustion. At this point Cassia didn't care.

She was sick of looking at the stuff and just wanted to take it all in the house so she could collapse on her bed and rest.

"I'm going to start the thing just to make sure the battery doesn't die from having the doors open so much," Genevieve called to Cassia, swinging the rental truck's huge bundle of keys.

Cassia waved acknowledgment while continuing to gather papers that somehow had escaped their boxes.

Genevieve squawked incoherently from inside the cab of the rental truck and then emerged a moment later with a black phone that looked slightly damaged on one corner. "Guess what I found under the driver's seat when I went to go adjust it?" Genevieve asked.

Cassia groaned. All that work, and the phone had been in the cab the entire time.

"Tell me again why we were looking so hard for that phone?" Genevieve said over a plate of pimento loaf sandwich in the kitchen. They had straightened up a bit, but not put everything back into the pantry. Genevieve had wanted to go into the weird basement area at least one more time and search for anything else of interest. She had already found a hole to the outside that she thought the mice were coming in. A ball of steel wool shoved in the hole later, and Cassia's problems were just down to finding the mice already in the house.

Oh, yeah, and the murder of Owen Mensky.

Which really shouldn't be her problem except jumpy Sheriff Andrews thought she might be involved due to the random coincidence of a rental truck.

Genevieve stared at Cassia. "Hello? Earth to Cassia? Are you in there?"

Cassia focused on the present. "Yeah, sorry. It's been a long week."

"Yes, it has. I've been there with you for most of it."

She had, Cassia realized.

Cassia tried to explain to Genevieve about her run-in with David Clyders and Kai, but it came out as a jumbled mess. Genevieve finally raised her eyebrows in understanding.

"So, you wanted to find the phone and give it to David so he wouldn't try to find your house and come and get it?"

"Right," Cassia said.

"But if you give it to him, he'll know you had it, and if he's been tracking it, he'll know it was at your house, or some place you parked the moving truck at."

Dang it, she had a point, Cassia realized with a sinking feeling in her gut. How could she get David his phone back without him knowing where it had been? Or if it was too late for that…

What could she do?

Did it matter?

Maybe he was totally innocent in all this and she was over-thinking it.

On the other hand, someone was dead. Perhaps better safe than sorry was the way to go with this one.

Cassia frowned. She was too tired to solve this problem tonight. "Let's talk about this tomorrow. Are you still off?"

"Yup, no work tomorrow," Genevieve said, taking a huge bite of her sandwich like it was a totally normal day.

Even Miss Mansfield was in the kitchen, much happier with Cassia now that her routine of eating at her special desk was back. Cassia made a note that a cat's pout lasts as long as the routine was interrupted, but didn't seem to go beyond that. Nice to know.

"Good," Cassia said. "Spend it with me. Maybe we can go hit Roger up for a metal detector before going back to the storage space."

That brought a familiar glint to Genevieve's eyes. "Good idea. I think that will be a lot of fun. Maybe we can even convince him to come with us and see what he can do about the security system."

"Or the map," Cassia said. She had forgotten about the map until just that moment. She needed to go and see how crumpled it was in her backpack. Maybe she could make a copy and they could put the original back in the bear and no one would be the wiser.

Why hadn't she done that in the first place? Cassia bit her

lip. Realizing the best thing to do after the fact was getting a bit old.

She took a big bite of her sandwich and chewed rapidly, as if she could crunch her problems away with her teeth. What had started as a simple matter of moving stuff back into the mansion was turning out to be more complicated than she could have ever imagined ahead of time.

Perhaps Nate would have some good news for her tomorrow.

CHAPTER 19

No, Nate did not have any good news for her.

Cassia's no-good week was getting into the just rotten territory.

Cassia sat in front of Nate Perauski in his law office, having already run the gauntlet of getting change for the meters at the K-Okay convenience store just outside of town, finding a parking spot, and surviving the disapproving look of Deloras Anderson in the law office lobby.

Nate sat across from her, looking vaguely apologetic, although Cassia knew none of this was his fault directly.

"What do you mean, they rescheduled again?" Cassia asked. The law firm in New York was slipperier than a fish in an icehouse, a saying she'd learned from Genevieve. Why was it so hard for them to keep their meetings?

"I don't know," he said. He started to say something several times, stopping himself each time.

"What?" Cassia asked. If there was something weird going on, she needed to know about it.

"It's just that I get this feeling they are waiting for some-thing. Every time they call to reschedule, the guy on the other end just hangs on the phone, as if he's waiting for me to say something specific. After a moment or two, he just excuses himself and hangs up."

"You mean like a code word or something?" Cassia asked.

He turned a little red. "Sounds crazy when you say it, I know, but yeah. I just get that sense."

Great.

Isn't it enough she found their contact information and the string of digits that was the speed of light written underneath it?

"The speed of light numbers didn't work?" Cassia asked.

"No. I tried once. Honestly, I felt like an idiot. But no, that wasn't what he was looking for. He just excused himself again."

Okay, Aunt Mildred, you might have actually made this puzzle too hard for your niece, Cassia thought.

What else could it be?

Then Cassia realized she had another eleven months in this place anyhow. She might as well work at solving this problem. That is, she had eleven months if she wasn't hauled off to jail.

"Have you heard anything about the Owen Mensky investigation?" Cassia asked.

"No, not directly. Though I doubt Sheriff Andrews is making a point to keep me in the loop. Or even wanting me to know anything," Nate said. He smoothed down his tie and then looked into his now empty coffee cup. Their coffees together were beginning to be a routine.

"They wouldn't tell you first if they were going to come and try to arrest me again, would they?" Cassia asked, not really thinking so, but it might be worth asking about.

"They most decidedly would not," Nate said. "Our guys are pretty good, but that doesn't mean they want a lawyer there making sure their suspect doesn't talk."

Suspect. Oh, how much she hated that word.

"Okay. Good point. Not good for me, but you know what I

mean," Cassia said in a rush. She sort of didn't want to leave his office, since that would make their failure to learn anything more from the New York firm feel a bit more real.

Plus Sheriff Andrews was out there, looking for a suspect, and always seeming to see Cassia as one.

"Sorry," Nate said, shrugging. "If I could do anything, I would. The best thing for you is to just focus on what you need for the mansion. That tape of the other truck being on the grounds was a lucky break for you indeed."

Indeed.

"Okay, thanks," Cassia said, rising from her chair. "I'll see if I can find any supersecret code words or something lying around the house."

Nate stood too. "I don't think whatever it is will be just any old thing. Ms. Mandress was a pretty sharp cookie, and she seems to have known a lot about your interests. I'll bet it is something that she thinks you in particular would find."

Cassia paused at that. A month ago, she would have scoffed at such a statement, but the more she learned about her aunt, the more she tended to agree with Nate's statement. She'd have to keep that in mind when searching.

It was another beautiful late autumn day in Forbidden Valley. The sun streamed down on Main Street. The messiness of the fall leaves had long ago been taken care of by the townspeople, leaving the boulevard pristine and almost festive.

The five-and-dime had already put up Thanksgiving decorations, even though the holiday was weeks away. Cassia especially liked the colored paper turkeys and the paper chains. That was the sort of decorations she'd made as a kid. Her mom had liked to tease Cassia by turning half the loops into Möbius strips, something that would make kid-Cassia scream bloody murder. Now she wanted all her paper chains to be Möbius strips, infinite loops of paper that would forever remind her of her mother.

Cassia pulled down her green wool captain's hat and pulled in her coat. Beautiful or not, the wind still chilled her. Rather than face her still rough parallel parking skills, Cassia decided to walk over to the diner where she was meeting Genevieve and not take the time to move her car to the rear parking lot. It was worth the extra seventy-five cents in meter fees to not have to worry about dinging Deloras's antique baby blue Chevy coupe just yet, though she'd have to move the car eventually.

Since the diner didn't serve breakfast, it was deserted at 10:30 in the morning on a Monday. Cassia entered with a ring of the bells hanging from the door. Genevieve sat at the counter, a plate in front of her, and lifting a forkful of something topped with whipped cream. Whatever it was looked delicious.

Interrupted by the noise, Genevieve looked over at the door and gave Cassia a big smile. "Come! Trent made us pie. *Walnut* pie. It's soooo good."

Cassia laughed. She wanted to tease Genevieve about her love of food, but honestly she loved pie more, so she bit her tongue and just walked over and took the stool next to Genevieve.

"Morning, Cassia," Trent said, standing abruptly from behind the counter where he'd been digging around in the lower shelving. He held a stack of rarely used serving dishes they normally stored on the bottom shelf.

Cassia jumped back, her hand over her heart. "You can't do that!" she said.

Trent looked down at the dishes and then back to Cassia, confused. "Get plates?"

"Scare me," Cassia said, the ridiculousness of her statement sinking in. "Sorry, my bad. I didn't know you were there."

"No problem," Trent said. "I know just the cure." He gave her a wicked smile before taking a regular plate over to the pie caddy and cutting her a massive piece of the dark walnut pie. It looked like nuts set in sugary goo. It looked fantastic.

"Whip creme?" he asked, pulling a silver bowl from the cooler.

Cassia nodded.

He scooped a huge mound of white fluffy cream from the bowl and dumped it on the plate, almost completely covering the pie.

Cassia felt a wave of love for the man.

One forkful later, and she was in heaven.

Trent chuckled and went into the back since neither Genevieve nor Cassia seemed much interested in anything but eating their pie. All too soon it was gone. Despite getting a huge piece, Cassia stared longingly at the pie caddy.

"So, what did Nate say?" Genevieve asked, pulling Cassia out of her pie-obsessed thoughts.

"Nothing good," Cassia said. At Genevieve's startled look, she clarified. "Oh, I'm not going back to jail or anything that he knows of... it's just those people in New York seem to be playing games, and I don't even know the rules."

"Yeah, that doesn't sound good alright."

Just then, the door opened and Roger came in. His white hair was tucked under a pin-striped painter's cap, and he wore a huge, colorful crocheted scarf wrapped around his neck and covering half his face.

"Wow, nice scarf," Genevieve called.

Roger nodded and unwrapped the scarf, revealing his smile. "Mrs. Jenson gave it in exchange for some help with her fancy new doorbell. She told me this is what I get for not telling her what color I wanted."

Nice. Cassia could get behind that sort of thinking. Mrs. Jenson did fantastic work. Despite having yarn strands in a wild array of blue, yellow, orange, red, gray, and green, the whole thing worked. Roger looked like he was wearing a representation of spring on his neck.

Roger sat down next to Cassia, just as Trent came back in from the back holding a plate with a fish-shaped walnut tart on it.

Cassia gasped.

Genevieve elbowed Cassia. "That was my idea. What do you think?"

"That you're a genius," Cassia said.

Roger rubbed his hands together in anticipation. "I agree. Whatever you want, you can have."

Trent slid the pie in front of Roger, who wasted no time pulling a fork from a nearby napkin bundle.

"Ah, that was amazing, Trent," Roger said as he slid the now empty dish away. Trent took it with a small bow and put it in the bus bin under the counter.

"Trent," Cassia said before he could disappear in the back again. "I found David's phone in the moving truck. He said to bring it here. He wouldn't give me another number to call or way to contact him…" Cassia trailed off on the last part, hoping Trent would take the bait and give some information. She pushed the phone across the counter to Trent.

He reached for the phone. "That's weird. That phone number is the only thing I have too," Trent said. "Guess that explains why he hasn't been picking up."

Okay, that wasn't helpful.

Trent turned again to go into the back.

"How well do you know him?" Cassia called after him.

Trent turned back to her. "Not all that well, I guess. He always seemed like a stand-up guy, if a little on the blunt side, but that never bothered me much." Trent glanced at Genevieve, and Roger before turning back to Cassia. "Has something bad happened?"

"I don't know," Cassia said. "I just thought it a little weird how he *knew* he'd left his phone in the truck."

"Maybe he went there to make a call in private and just forgot to grab it again until after. I do that all the time because my phone is so honking big," Trent said. "It's stuck on the shelf in the back right now."

Oh. That could explain it.

Cassia looked at Genevieve, who shrugged. They hadn't thought of that. Of course, they usually had bags for stuff like that. Men shoved everything into their pants.

Once Trent disappeared into the back, Genevieve clapped her hands to get their attention.

"Alright, we're all fueled up. Let's hit the road," Genevieve said. "I want to get out of here before Bridget comes in. Sometimes she asks me to cover on Mondays at the last minute and I don't wanna today."

"I'm ready," Roger said.

Cassia raised her eyebrows. She'd missed something here.

Genevieve caught her confusion. "Forgot to tell ya, Roger said he did have a metal detector and he was down for an adventure today. He told me this morning when you were at the lawyer's."

Roger curled his fingers in anticipation. "My old multifrequency one was going out, so I've tried to rig up my own design for a pulse induction unit. I've just been waiting for a good field test."

Multifrequency? Pulse induction? Cassia looked at Genevieve. Genevieve just shook her head. She didn't know either.

"Whatever you've got is way more than what we've got," Genevieve said, grabbing Roger by the arm to encourage him to make his way to the door. "To the treasure!" Genevieve called as they reached the door and exited.

Cassia followed, excited and a little nervous at what those two were going to do at the storage space today.

CHAPTER 20

The sun slanted into Cassia's windshield, blinding her temporarily until she pulled the shade down. Even though it was just past 1 pm, the sun didn't get that high in the sky in early November.

Next to her, Genevieve was still pulling open every compartment in Cassia's car and testing out all the goodies. She'd stopped fiddling with the radio (satellite radio, apparently) when Cassia had squawked that she couldn't concentrate on the road with all that racket.

Genevieve had reluctantly turned down the 80s music Cassia recognized from old movies. "You're no fun sometimes."

"What?" Cassia said, glancing at Genevieve before turning into the Mucho Junk parking lot. "How can you say that?"

"You won't wear my clothes that I *custom make*. You don't want to listen to tunes—"

"It's not that," Cassia said, trying to keep from clenching her jaw. "It's that I can't afford to get into an accident with this car. I've never had anything so nice."

"You're not going to get into an accident," Genevieve said

reassuringly just as Cassia turned into a space and misjudged the depth of the spot. They bounced back from the cement tire stops. Genevieve just smiled at Cassia. "See, didn't even scrape the bottom or anything." She poked Cassia in the arm. "No rust for you, young lady."

Rust?

"Rust?" Cassia asked, but Genevieve had turned her attention to gathering her things from the seat and floor around her and shoving them back into her backpack.

"Rust?" Cassia asked again.

"Rust," Genevieve said. "You know, from all the salt they put down in winter. If you scrape up your car, you get rust in the spot you damaged." She giggled at Cassia's horrified look. "Just don't scrape up your car."

Great. Another thing not to do. Would she have to pay back any damage if she didn't manage to make it through the year's probation that her aunt had put in the will? Things don't rust that fast... do they?

"Wait," Cassia said as the door slammed and snapped her out of her reverie. Genevieve was already outside and standing next to the car, waiting for Roger to arrive.

That morning, taking one look at Cassia's new car, Roger had insisted on driving himself in his own truck since he'd last used one of his detectors in a muddy field. Genevieve promptly claimed payback after that and said Cassia could drive both of them in Cassia's car for once, since Roger didn't have room in the cab of his truck to take them too. Or rather, he didn't have a seat. For some reason, the passenger bucket seat of his truck was in his house for repairs.

Cassia didn't ask why. She knew better.

"What a beautiful day," Genevieve said. She stretched and yawned in the fall sunlight, then turned her stretch into a wave to a woman at the far end of the parking lot. The woman scowled at them and then scurried up the stairs to one of the smaller storage spaces there, disappearing with a flick of her dowdy blue dress. Other than Cassia's car, the woman's brown wreck of a car was the only other vehicle there.

"Friendly," Cassia said.

"Maybe she's just in a hurry," Genevieve said, ever the optimist.

A few seconds later, Roger's van rolled into the parking lot, quieter than Cassia expected. His red cargo van with round submarine windows was definitely out of the seventies, but Roger must have made some improvements to the thing because it was almost as silent as an electric car.

Maybe it was electric. With Roger, one never knew.

Pulling up next to Cassia's car, Roger parked and got out. Opening one of the back doors, he gestured to the equipment laying on the floor in the rear. "Behold my beauties," he said, beaming with pride.

Inside the van lay two metal detectors. At least Cassia could figure that out. One looked lighter and had a flat paddle coil at the bottom. It looked like something she'd seen the strange guys who always combed the beaches in LA carry. The second detector was something else entirely. It was huge, for one thing, with a harness that went over one's shoulders but was stiff enough to keep a person's shape even when no one was wearing it. Then there was the bottom of its pole. Instead of a neat little detector, it had a large three-spoke wheel that would have been large enough to be a car wheel.

"Wow, is that your custom deal?" Cassia asked and pointed to the huge one.

"Yup. I could have made it smaller with a detached battery, but haven't gotten that far yet." He pulled on the harness, and even he had to give it some effort to lift it. "Don't worry," he said between grunts. "I'll get this one. You guys get the other one and shut the door."

Some lifting and fussing later, Cassia and Genevieve had

pulled out the other detector, which was heavier than it looked, shut the van door, and motioned Roger to follow them around to the back. The gopher holes were still there.

Roger gave a low whistle. "That is some mess. It looks like someone's already been here."

"Yup," Genevieve said. "But they didn't have your gear."

Roger perked up with the praise. He set down the massive detector and went closer to one of the holes, a neat pile of dirt still sitting next to it. He peered into it. Looking around, he found a long stick and then poked it into the hole. It kept going in and he leaned over, pushing until his wrist was inside the hole.

"Deep. If that's how far they're looking, that one won't do." He nodded at the detector Genevieve and Cassia carried between the two of them.

"Oh thank goodness," Genevieve said as she abruptly dropped the bottom end of the detector. Cassia nearly fell over with the surprise shift of her end of the load. She stumbled and righted herself, and gave Roger a weak smile as he looked up, concerned.

"Don't worry, we won't break anything," Cassia said to him, then glared back at Genevieve.

"Oh, right, sorry, slipped," Genevieve said.

Cassia made a great show of putting her end down gently, then stood next to Roger at the edge of the hole. "Why won't that one work?" she asked.

"That one only goes down a few inches. Six at the most. For something this deep, you need a commercial level pulse detector. They cost a pretty penny, which is why I made my own." He stood and rubbed his hands excitedly. "This will be a true challenge."

Cassia rubbed her itchy eye, and only made it worse as bits of gritty dirt smeared on her face, making her eyes water and blink. The hot sun now didn't feel so friendly, rather a hot nuisance that made her long for shade and a lemonade.

They'd found an unattacked stretch of ground and helped Roger wave his detector over it. Nothing for quite a few minutes, until a low buzzing sound came from his equipment. "I'd always disliked the harsh squawk of metal detectors, so came up with something different," he said. The something different was so low pitched, Cassia thought she could feel the sound with her toes.

The first signal had been exciting.

It had yielded exactly one disgustingly dirty steel-toed boot with half a rotting shoelace.

The second time had also been exciting, except it had gained them nothing but shovels full of red dirt. "Iron oxide," Roger said after close inspection. "Not our normal dirt here."

"You mean someone brought it in," Genevieve said.

"Maybe." Roger shrugged.

"Wait," Cassia said, confused. "Why would someone bring in dirt?"

"Because it sets off metal detectors," Genevieve said. Her smirk revealed she thought it was a pretty good prank.

Pretty good, except it was getting in their way of finding anything useful.

Cassia huffed, but tucked her hair behind her ear and kept digging where Roger motioned to. He'd had the foresight to bring shovels and gloves. Too bad he was too busy using the detector to help them use them.

After several more false alarms that pulled up another boot, an unidentified piece of metal piping, a painted blue box containing more red dirt, and a few very rusty garden tools from roughly fifty years ago, Cassia had had enough. Her back ached, the sheen of sweat coating her now feeling clammy in the breeze coming up with the setting sun, and they'd found exactly nothing good.

All they'd done was make their own set of holes next to the ones already out there.

Cassia walked to where Genevieve and Roger were sitting on the edge of the field, taking a break. "Do you think this entire thing is a joke?" Cassia asked, motioning to the field behind them.

"Looks like it," Genevieve said, unperturbed. She grabbed her backpack and pulled open the main compartment and pulled out three wax paper-wrapped sandwiches. "Tuna for you, you, and me," she said as she handed out the welcome goodies.

"You made snacks?" Cassia asked inanely as she took the sandwich. It felt soggy and heavy, and she was so happy to have it.

"Even brought drinks, although they are probably a bit warm," Genevieve said as she pulled out three root beers from her backpack. Cassia could have kissed her.

She sat down with a thump next to Genevieve to eat her lunch. The tuna still had just a hint of coolness. The root beer was sweet and stinging with carbonation. It was glorious.

Suddenly, Cassia could see the humor in the situation. "Maybe we should have used the map."

"Map?" Roger perked up. "You have a map? Why didn't you say so?"

Cassia and Genevieve exchanged glances. Cassia could feel the heat of her face turning red. Yes, why hadn't she said so many shovelfuls of dirt earlier?

"That's not much of a map," Roger said as he peered over Cassia's shoulder at the smeared and scribbled paper she held out.

"No, that's sort of what we thought," Cassia said, feeling disappointed despite herself. Roger was so good at so many things. Somehow she thought he'd figure out this mess of a map.

"I think those are houses," Genevieve said, pointing to strange structures with the triangle.

Roger tilted his head this way and that. "They could be. They remind me of something."

Hope sprang into Cassia's chest.

"That looks like an old soviet map I saw in one of my magazines. That symbol wasn't for houses, though."

"No? What was it for?" Cassia asked, too impatient to just wait for his answer.

But Roger was not to be rushed. After much staring at it, he finally focused back on her. "Antennas. They were for huge power antennas."

"Wait, what? There are so many of them. Where would there be that many power lines?" Cassia asked.

Genevieve raised her eyebrows and pointed to the far side of the building. Just peeking over the roof, Cassia spied the top of an enormous power tower, one of many that ran along the freeway.

CHAPTER 21

Cassia, Genevieve, and Roger stood on the little hill in front of the storage space complex, staring at the line of power transmission towers that accompanied the freeway off into the distance. The low, late fall sun glinted off the soaring metal beams hundreds of feet above the freeway, making them almost look like enormous golden men marching off into the distance. Cassia had never really paid attention to them before, but they were almost beautiful in their strange resemblance to tall stick men. Really huge stick men.

"There are so many of them, and they all look the same!" Genevieve said. Cassia had to agree with her. She looked down at her copy of the map and tried to turn it this way and that. Nothing seemed to match the scrawled layout. Roger and Genevieve did the same with the photos they'd taken of the map with their phones. The silence said no one was having much luck figuring it out.

"Are you sure those symbols stand for power towers?" Cassia asked Roger.

He lowered his phone. "Well, I can't be sure, for sure, since I didn't make that map. I'm just telling you what I remember seeing. Maybe we should get back and see if we can look for matching images on the interwebs."

"You're not doing an image search of the whole map," Cassia said, alarmed.

Roger's hurt expression pricked at Cassia.

"No, of course not," Roger said. "I'm not going to put it up there to possibly be stored by those search engines."

"I didn't mean—" Cassia said, but then got distracted by a white car coming up the service road to the storage complex. It looked familiar, but she wasn't sure. The car turned into the storage complex's driveway, revealing the driver's spring-like brown curls.

"Genevieve," Cassia said, cutting in front of Roger to grab Genevieve's arm. "That's the woman who owned the bear… owns the bear, and all that other stuff."

"The bear?" Genevieve looked down at Cassia's hands. "And the map inside it?"

Cassia nearly jumped. Yes, the map. An electric wave passed over her scalp. The map she was holding right that minute and probably wasn't even supposed to know existed. She nearly crumpled the map into a ball to hide it, but at the last minute forced herself to slow down and fold it.

"Yes. That too," Cassia said, pacing and clenching the map. "We should talk to her. She might know something about Owen Mensky's death. She might have seen something."

"Good idea," Genevieve said. They watched the car turn left into the far parking lot. "You know what would be the perfect icebreaker?"

Cassia shook her head.

"Giving her stuff back," Genevieve said.

Cassia glanced at the map. Genevieve followed her eyes.

"Don't worry about that," Genevieve said. "We've got pictures and…" Genevieve walked to where she'd stashed her backpack and grabbed it. Digging around in it, she pulled out a small yellowed envelope with thread hanging out of it. "And I've got my emergency sewing kit. Let's get her stuff together."

The time to dig the storage space key out of her bag seemed to stretch on forever. Cassia thought she could almost feel the woman's presence at the far end of the complex, pulling at her. They had to hurry or the woman would come and go before they even got Cassia's storage space open. Finally, the lock gave with a click and Cassia threw open the door, nearly hitting Roger, who had chosen rather poorly to stand too close behind.

While Genevieve ran in to grab the bear from where they'd stashed it inside the desk and shoved the map inside before sewing away, Cassia struggled with the garage door. Roger helped. Between the two of them, they managed to finally work the metal door loose and send it flying up on its rails. It would be easier to get the rest of that woman's forgotten items out the large door, Cassia told herself, ignoring the tense anxiety in her gut with the stuffy air in the space, and the knowledge someone had been crushed to death just one space over.

Someone she actually knew.

Not that she knew him all that much, but in all fairness, it was as much as she wanted to know him. Still, dead was dead, and being dead was creepy as all get-out.

"Don't you have any bags or something?" Roger asked as he tried to keep from dropping what looked like half a pet store of cat toys—a red feather on a long pole, several crinkling balls, a misshapen stuffed tiger. He also balanced a set of long strips of wood paneling and an old yellow fondue set with a woman with a sixties blond flip hairdo and a huge smile posing on the box.

Genevieve and Cassia were similarly loaded, except Genevieve had the prized bear too and was trying to pull off acting like it was just another object in the pile.

"No, sorry," Cassia called back to him. "I wasn't really thinking about packing up her stuff, though I suppose I should have."

Cassia led the way across the parking lot. She could still see the woman's white car parked on the other side of the complex. They hadn't taken too long. Cassia tried to squelch the hope rising in her chest. The last thing she needed was to act weird and manic in front of the woman.

It turned out to be too late to stop that from happening. Going too fast and looking down to catch a falling cat toy, Cassia didn't notice the woman turning the corner ahead and nearly walked into her. As it was, Cassia dropped most of the things she was carrying.

The woman jumped back at the sight of the three of them coming at her, her brown curls bouncing. She stared at them warily, then looked down at the pile at Cassia's feet and gasped.

"Hi," Cassia said awkwardly. The woman didn't look up. "Yeah, that's your stuff."

The woman looked up at that, her expression more closed than it had been a moment before.

"No," Cassia added in a rush, "I didn't steal it. I mean, I didn't mean to." She motioned at the stuff Genevieve and Roger held. "All this fell out of your car. I thought you might want it again, but didn't know how to get ahold of you, especially after…" Especially after the caretaker kicked the bucket. Cassia bit her lip to keep *that* from slipping out.

"Oh," the woman said. "Oh!" she said more loudly when she bent down and picked up a particularly ratty stuffed rabbit with one ear missing and a dirty gray streak on one side. "Muffin will be so happy. And so will Edgar. He never stopped giving me a hard time about losing Muffin's best toy."

Roger, Genevieve, and Cassia stared at the absolute wreck that was Muffin's best toy.

The woman didn't even notice as she kept prattling on about each item in the pile. It seemed she knew them all in graphic detail and probably could have given the dates of construction for each one. It was an odd contrast of organized details as compared to the cloud of chaos and tears she'd been when Cassia had seen her the first time.

It probably helped that there was no Owen Mensky there yelling at the poor woman, addling her concentration and well-being.

The wonderful Owen Mensky, who was the whole reason they were there trying to get more information.

Cassia cleared her throat. "So, um—"

"So, who is Muffin?" Genevieve said loudly, talking over Cassia as she stepped forward and swung her arm around Cassia's shoulder, neatly pulling her back so firmly Cassia nearly fell.

"Oh Muffin is my handsome Savannah boy. He loves playing fetch, and hide, and…"

Roger leaned in to Cassia and whispered in her ear. "Is Muffin a child or a pet?"

Cassia shook her head. She had no idea. Genevieve, though, was having no problem acting fascinated and as if she could understand the woman's rambling story perfectly. Of course, Genevieve would never act so gauche as to ask if Muffin had two legs or four.

"I'm sure Muffin probably missed this beautiful creature then," Genevieve said, holding out the pristine white bear. Even knowing it had been cut open, Cassia could not find the seam on it. Genevieve did good work.

The woman looked at the bear blankly, then back up at Genevieve. "That's not mine."

That even took Genevieve by surprise. "Not yours?"

The woman shook her head.

"But I found it with all of your other stuff out in the parking lot," Cassia said, speaking despite Genevieve's look telling her to stay out of it.

"Maybe someone threw it away," the woman said with a shrug as she opened her large handbag and started stuffing ratty toys inside of it. "It's too big for Muffin, and I certainly don't have a use for stuffed bears."

Cassia and Genevieve exchanged glances over the woman's head as she was gathering her things. Cassia wasn't sure what Genevieve's look meant, but she knew her own meant *now what?*

"You must be happy to no longer have to deal with that mean caretaker," Roger's low voice said. All three women turned to look at him at once.

"What do you mean?" the woman said, with a look of complete innocence.

"The dead guy," Roger said. Cassia stared at him. She had a sudden warm feeling at for once not being the most clueless person in the room. Is this what she did when other people gave her such strange looks?

The woman was staring at Roger too. "What dead guy?" she asked, her voice so low and quiet it was difficult to hear.

"Owen Mensky. The caretaker," Roger said, barrelling on and not noticing the blood draining from the woman's face. "Smashed like a bug. His ears stuffed with cigars and everything."

The woman screamed.

CHAPTER 22

"Way to go, Roger," Genevieve said as she threw a piece of dead grass away. "I haven't seen a woman that upset in years."

Roger blushed but said nothing as he leaned back, resting his hands on the dirt behind him and pretending to be totally engrossed with something in the distance. The ground was cold and chill, but not one of them was ready to leave the storage complex yet. That would be admitting defeat.

And the day certainly had tried to defeat them.

Instead, they sat out on the small hill next to the parking lot that overlooked the highway and the long trail of transmission towers leading off into the distance.

Tried as they might with the woman from earlier, they had not managed to get another coherent word out of her. After a seemingly endless moment of screaming, she stopped to inhale again and Genevieve managed to whisper something reassuring in her ear. Cassia was going to have to figure out what that was since Cassia was sure she'd lose her hearing before the screeching stopped, and then, just like that, it did stop, thanks to Genevieve.

After that, the woman led them in a daze to her car and let

them hand her the items they carried, which she took from them and shoved roughly in the back seat, pushing and cramming it in so she could slam the door. Then she promptly got in and drove away before anyone could stop her.

Instead, they watched helplessly as the white car disappeared in the darkening evening.

"Did anyone think to get her license plate?" Cassia asked.

Roger and Genevieve both shook their heads.

Some investigation. Cassia kicked at the ground ahead of her.

"It's worse," Genevieve said. Dreading the answer, but unable to bring herself to stop Genevieve from talking, Cassia stared at her friend.

"She took the bear. The one she said wasn't hers."

"The one with the map in it," Roger pointed out needlessly. They all knew it had the map in it. Hopefully, the woman herself would never find out its existence.

But why had she taken it?

As if to answer Cassia's question, Genevieve said, "She was in shock. She was just taking everything. We shouldn't have handed it to her."

Cassia had to give Genevieve credit. At least she didn't look at Roger and make him feel even worse when she said that.

Of course, any one of them could have had the foresight to keep it the moment the woman said it wasn't hers.

But none of them had.

"I'm sure it was with her other stuff that had fallen out of her car," Cassia said, still confused about the situation. "It's not like there are a ton of people out here anyhow," she gestured to the complex in the middle of nowhere, "especially not ones randomly dropping things."

"You said she was really upset that day, right?" Genevieve asked.

"Yes. I was surprised she could even drive. Mensky was yelling at her like no tomorrow for taking her things out of the storage when she was behind on her rent. He told her that was a condition of her rental…" Cassia trailed off and stopped. Something didn't make sense, unless…unless it made complete sense.

Cassia turned to Roger. "You said Mensky was going into people's storage spaces without their permission."

He nodded slowly.

"And taking things."

Roger nodded again.

Cassia leaned in. "Did he ever put strange things *into* their spaces?"

Roger's eyebrows shot up.

"I mean," Cassia said, speaking her just discovered theory out loud to see if it made as much sense to them as it did in her head, "what if you wanted to store something without anyone knowing it was yours? Wouldn't it be the perfect place? A whole array of rental spaces and you have complete control over the ones behind on their rent."

"Cat, you are a genius for sure," Genevieve said, followed by a whoop. "I bet that's it."

Cassia smirked despite herself.

Cassia wasn't feeling so smug several hours later when she finally made it home after dropping Genevieve off at her car and driving the long way back to the mansion in the dark. It wasn't even 8 pm yet. It shouldn't feel like midnight in some scary book about the Moors, but it did. Cassia gripped the steering wheel even tighter as she passed the empty moving truck parked on the front lawn to go back to the pitch-black rear of the house where the garage was. Another thing to fix when the money situation was taken care of. Women do not park in dark spots. Ever.

Not if they can help it.

Her mood didn't improve when she opened the front door to see the hallway stuffed with goods from the moving truck. Much of it had found its way to the rooms upstairs, but in the end, she and Genevieve had been too tired to take all of it up the stairs, and the last boxes had been stashed along the long hallway of the entryway leading to the kitchen.

Shutting the front door firmly, Cassia abruptly sneezed. Apparently, they'd brought in all the dust that had been on the boxes too. A fine layer of it now coated the glossy wood floor. Cat paw prints revealed where Miss Mansfield had paced near the narrow windows that edged the massive front door.

"And I thought she didn't care," Cassia said, eyeing the line of prints. They probably led to some now dirty yellow linen furniture. People who buy light colored furniture must be the same exact people who can afford help to clean the furniture, and floors, and everything else. A set of people that didn't include her, at least for now.

"Meow." Miss Mansfield appeared in the kitchen doorway and made her way quickly to Cassia, snaking between her legs as a greeting.

"Well, hello to you, too. Have a good day?" Cassia asked.

Miss Mansfield stared at her with her golden eyes, not saying a word.

"Right. No answer. How about, do you want dinner?"

"Meow."

Of course, Miss Mansfield answered that one. How unusual would it be for a cat to understand English perfectly?

After dinner for her and the cat, Cassia sat in the library. It'd been a while since she'd allowed herself the luxury of going into that room full of precious astronomy books, and the physical proof that she did have family that was like her and she wasn't a crazy one-off. Senior Mandress had loved astronomy as much as she had, or more, judging by the huge and costly library of books he'd accumulated, not to mention the custom telescope built off the back of the house.

Cassia stared at the books. She'd gone through a significant chunk of them looking for more notes from her aunt, but hadn't found any yet.

"Okay, Universe, give me a clue that I need," Cassia said out loud as she walked to one of the far shelves by the window and pulled a jewel blue book at random. *Quantum Dynamics.* Well, okay, not one of Cassia's strongest subjects, even if she did love the weirdness of it.

Taking the book back to one of the long tables that reminded Cassia of a library, she flipped through the pages, looking at the diagrams full of lines and wiggles and formulas written out in Greek letters and symbols. This book was old, and used the old-fashioned notation, not the more modern matrixes they'd used in Cassia's classes. It looked even more intimidating and incomprehensible that way.

Flipping through every page, Cassia reached the end of the book with a sigh and flipped it shut. No note from her aunt. No underlined words making things clearer for her.

Perhaps the Universe wasn't in the listening mood. Miss Mansfield jumped on the table and nudged Cassia, rubbing her furry face on Cassia's until Cassia pet her. Maybe the cat did like her after all.

The excitement of the day and the long fruitless hours of digging behind the Mucho Junk finally sank in. Cassia yawned and left the library, turning the corner as she flipped the switch. Just at that moment, Miss Mansfield ran out past her, tripping up Cassia's feet and sending her flying into the stack of banker's boxes lined against the wall. Cassia, the boxes, and their spilled contents landed in a tumble all over the wood floor.

"Ouch." Cassia pulled in her leg and examined her stinging knee. No blood, but it hurt like she'd done some damage. Tears welled in her eyes at the pain.

Dabbing at her eyes, Cassia took a deep breath and willed the pain to ease. She was too old to feel sorry for herself. She refused.

Once she could see clearly again, she surveyed the mess around her. Among the spilled papers were some smaller photographs. She'd not seen those before. Genevieve must have checked that box and not thought it important to mention to Cassia since it wasn't the phone they were looking for.

Cassia pulled the photos towards her, sifting through the papers to find them all. Most were black and white, and cut all different sizes, with a few color ones thrown in. She recognized her grandfather and aunt in many of them, often amongst other people she didn't recognize, though none of the pictures were old as the one of her aunt they'd found in the hidden room. A few of the images even looked like they were from the eighties judging by the big shoulder pads and even bigger hair styles of the women.

One of the photos of her grandfather caught her eye. He stood in front of an old stone building with towering columns, his suit jacket off. He had his arms around two young men on either side of him, one with a rounder face and a big cigar sticking out of his mouth, and the other long-faced, with stringy blond hair swooped across his forehead.

The blond reminded her of someone with his lopsided smile and strangely vacant expression.

Cassia gasped, as a bolt of electricity shot down her spine.

It reminded her of Kai Huntington.

Flipping the photograph over, Cassia searched for a date, but there was nothing. She ransacked through the photographs, but there were no others with the strange young man that looked just like Kai Huntington, but who couldn't have been him. The person in that photograph must be an old man by now, if not dead like her grandfather had been for many years.

She studied the photograph again in the low hallway light. The building took up most of the frame, and the top of the building where its name might have been written was cut off. It looked like an old and stately building—a courthouse, perhaps, in an enormous city like New York. There was nothing like that anywhere close to Forgotten Valley, Minnesota.

Maybe it went with some of the papers strewn about her. Cassia pulled a pile towards her when a motion caught her eye. The motion had been near the front door.

Her stomach leaden, Cassia slowly turned to stare at the front door. It stood shut and locked, like it always was when she was home alone. She was just about to turn back to her task when a black shape moved across one of the narrow windows beside the massive door, silhouetted by the overhead porch light.

There was someone outside, and they weren't knocking.

CHAPTER 23

A rush of fear passed over Cassia as she stared at the front door. She felt frozen in place, as if she moved one inch the person outside would know she was there, just feet away. Inches away.

The dim hallway light suddenly felt glaring and far too bright. Cassia wanted it off so she could hide in the darkness, but that would require her to move. And surely whoever was out there would notice less light coming out of the entry windows.

Miss Mansfield came back from the kitchen. Cassia felt Miss Mansfield's fur rubbing along her arms. She glanced down. The cat's eyes were big, with dilated pupils. Worse, she was absolutely silent, something that scared Cassia even more. If Miss Mansfield knew to be quiet, there must be danger.

Cassia slowly felt her pockets while she stared at the front door. A rush of relief hit her when she found her cell phone in one of them. She hadn't left it elsewhere for once. Fingers shaking, she dialed Genevieve's number. It was the most recent one on her call list.

It rang a few times, then, *"Hello,"* Genevieve said on the other end.

Cassia's tongue stuck in her throat. If someone was right there on the other side of the door, they would be able to hear her talk.

"Hello?" Genevieve said again.

Cassia forced herself to speak, whispering into the phone. "There is someone here."

"What?"

"There is someone here." Cassia tried again. It was just a whisper, but she felt like she was screaming. They must have heard her outside. Cassia's heart thumped in her chest, feeling like it was skipping a beat or two. She did not feel well.

"Cassia?" Genevieve asked, just as the door made a cracking sound as a body slammed into it.

Cassia screamed and scrambled to her feet, dropping the phone in her haste. Unthinking, she scrambled up the carpet covered stairs on all fours. Miss Mansfield rushed up ahead of her and ran down the second-floor landing to the left.

A second impact hit the front door. The frame cracked, and splinters flew into the hall entryway.

Cassia reached the top of the stairs and followed Miss Mansfield to the left. Then she realized her mistake.

Most of the doors were shut and locked. Out of sheer inertia, she'd not gotten around to unlocking most of the rooms after Sarah, her old housekeeper, had been arrested. The few rooms now unlocked were stuffed to the gills with stuff from the storage space.

Unable to think clearly with the sound of the door below finally giving way and smashing into the wall with the force of its opening, Cassia ran to the end of the hall and then up the stairway there that led to the third floor.

The third floor.

She should have run out the back of the house, not up.

Now she was trapped up high, and she hated heights. Worse yet, someone had already died falling from the roof after trying to take this exact same escape route.

Heavy feet clomped in the hallway. Boxes hit the wall as whoever was down there shoved them out of their way.

Cassia raced up the stairs to the third-floor landing of the tower room. Thankfully the doorknob turned in her hands. She let herself and Miss Mansfield in, then crouched in the darkness. Her ragged breath echoed off the walls of the small room. She tried to slow her breathing.

Miss Mansfield's wet nose nudged her arm. Cassia looked down. Miss Mansfield didn't make a sound. Instead, she jumped up to the windowsill, her dark form blocking what little light came in from the stars in the night sky.

Outside? Miss Mansfield wanted the window open?

While that felt like a good idea, if only to get away from the banging noises two stories away, it also felt like a really bad idea.

Falling from the roof might be just as fatal as whatever that person below had in mind.

After breaking down her door, it was clear they weren't there just for tea.

Hedging her bets, Cassia stood long enough to unlock the window that overlooked the rest of the house. It was about a ten-foot drop to the second-story roof since the only part of the house that had a third floor was the one room where she was standing.

Miss Mansfield rubbed insistently at Cassia's hand to open the window, but she wasn't going to do that. She didn't want Miss Mansfield out there either, not unless neither one of them had a choice.

The noises below tapered off, and then fell to silence. Cassia counted her heartbeats pulsing in her ears, but she had no sense of time.

What felt like ages later, she could hear someone calling her name. She crept to the door and cracked it open to listen. Maybe it was Genevieve. The room didn't have a window that overlooked the front drive, so it was impossible to see if another car had come.

The voice, while on the higher side, wasn't Genevieve's.

It was Kai Huntington's.

"Cassia!" he called. "Are you okay? Cassia, you chillin' here? I heard David was coming to the house and I rushed over here in case you needed me. He looked mighty upset."

David?

And Kai?

Were they both here?

David might lack in social skills, but would he really break down her door? And for why?

Kai kept calling, his southern California surfer's accent a weird contrast to the terrifying night.

"Cassia, I'm here to protect you, like a rad hero." Then a giggle. It sounded like he was on the second floor. Had he roamed all over the house to find her?

Crouching on the floor, Cassia held her breath. Hopefully he would give up and leave. She didn't want anyone to find her, unless it was Genevieve, or even the crabby sheriff. He might be a pain in the behind, but at least Cassia felt safe with him.

She didn't feel safe now.

A creak on the landing outside gave away too late that Kai hadn't given up his search for her. A second later, the door swung open, far too fast for her to reach the window and escape. She was blinded by the bright hallway light flooding in.

"There you are!" he said with a huge smile as he took two

steps and enveloped her in a tight hug as she stood. She pushed back, but he wouldn't let go.

"I'm fine," Cassia said, trying to get out of his arms, but it was like trying to move steel pinchers. How could such a scrawny guy be so strong?

"I'm so stoked I found you, girl," Kai said, as he loosened his grip and dropped one of his arms, but keeping Cassia close with his other. He stuck his thumb and pinky out on his free hand and wiggled it. Cassia still didn't know what that meant.

Its meaning certainly wasn't any clearer when he did it inches from her face.

"Let go of me," Cassia said. Her voice cracked and squeaked like a squeeze toy.

"I'm just so stoked you're alright," Kai said. He smiled down at her. His expression struck Cassia wrong. The smile didn't reach his eyes.

"I'm not alright," Cassia said through clenched teeth.

Miss Mansfield made a strange cat moan behind her, a mixture of unhappy and angry.

Startled, Kai glanced behind Cassia at Miss Mansfield.

Cassia took advantage of his distraction to lift her right foot and bring her heel down on his tennis shoe clad foot with all her might.

A sickening crunch came with the impact.

Kai yowled in pain. He released Cassia and she bolted for the door, Miss Mansfield leading the way.

Cassia took the stairs two at a time, letting the close walls of the staircase keep her upright as she careened down the two landings to the second floor. She ran down the main hallway to the central staircase.

"Ah, Cat, why'd you do that?" Kai called. "I'm trying to help you."

The central staircase seemed a mile ahead, even though Cassia knew it was only a few dozen yards.

"David is probably down there," Kai called. "Do you really want to face him? He's annngry."

More terror ripped at Cassia's heart.

No, she did not want to face David, but she wasn't sticking around to get grabbed by Kai again.

Rounding the corner at the top of the stairs, Cassia saw the wreck of the front door hanging open by one hinge. She peeked over the railing.

No David.

Kai's thundering steps echoed from the third-floor staircase behind her. She glanced back just as Kai exploded out of the stairway behind her and hit the far wall, going too fast to change his direction quickly.

He was faster than her.

She had to go!

Cassia bolted down the central staircase, hands on the railings. She only slipped once on the thick carpeting, but managed to stay upright and going forward.

Breaking her neck here would be game over.

The open door stood in front of her.

Then two headlights swung around the turnabout and shone into the mansion.

Was that a friend, or was it David, or someone else?

If Cassia guessed wrong, there was no help for miles and miles.

Miss Mansfield made Cassia's decision for her. Instead of bolting away, Miss Mansfield stood, waiting, in the entryway. When Cassia reached the bottom of the stairway, Miss Mansfield ran back to the kitchen and the rear of the house.

Not out the front door.

Cassia followed the cat. Not thinking. Barely able to draw enough breath.

Miss Mansfield made a beeline for the kitchen and then the pantry doors.

Luckily, Genevieve had not re-installed the false back of the pantry or the shelving. Cassia picked her way through the still disastrous kitchen and bolted inside the pantry. Miss Mansfield followed. The minute the tiny cat's tail cleared the door, Cassia pulled the pantry doors shut.

The cool draft of the open space behind her sent a shiver over Cassia's sweaty skin.

Miss Mansfield stood quietly at her feet, leaning her warm body against Cassia.

Cassia pressed an ear to the pantry door. Kai made it to the bottom of the stairway in a clatter of limbs, then ran from room to room on the first floor. His thunderous footsteps made it no mystery where he was.

Outside the mansion, a car door slammed.

What was going on?

Even from within the pantry, Cassia could hear running outside around the back of the house and by the kitchen door.

Someone slammed against the locked kitchen back door that faced the woods. Cassia jumped at the sudden noise.

Who was it?

More terrified of the chaos going on outside than the damp space behind her, Cassia backed up deeper into the tunnel from the pantry.

A gunshot rang out.

Biting back a scream, Cassia turned and bolted into the darkness for the stairs that led to the secret room below.

CHAPTER 24

The cool draft of the passageway now felt downright cold as Cassia hurried through the tunnel, feeling her way in the pitch-black. The passageway turned, and then she felt the narrow opening at the top of the stairs. Using both hands on the walls to brace herself, she made her way down, reaching for each step.

From the darkness below, Miss Mansfield let out a soft meow, letting Cassia know where she was.

Cassia quickened her pace, her anxiety ratcheting up with each creak of the old wood stairs.

Reaching the bottom, she turned and felt her way to the table under the stairs and crawled under it.

Now hidden, the enveloping black of the room felt reassuring.

Cassia waited for her eyes to adjust, but the room never got any brighter.

The quiet settled in over Cassia. Distant footsteps clomped above.

Just as Cassia calmed enough to feel her eyelids drooping in exhaustion, a crack of light filtered in from above. It was so faint Cassia wasn't sure if she was just imagining it.

Then it grew brighter.

Her heart skipped a beat.

Someone was coming.

Pushing further back into the space under the stairs, Cassia willed herself to become smaller.

It wasn't working.

She couldn't even get her feet completely under the stairs. Pulling with her hands on her ankles, she got as small as she possibly could. Someone would have to come all the way down and into the room to find her.

Miss Mansfield pressed up against her side.

They waited.

"Cassia," Kai called in a singsong voice. "You chillin' down there. I see some footsteps in this groovy space…"

His voice echoed off the walls in the tunnel above.

Slow footsteps coming closer echoed in the passageway. A beam of light swung, spilling down into the room where Cassia hid.

"This is pretty rad. If I had a mansion like this, I'd totally have hidden rooms too."

He almost sounded like he was talking to himself.

Cassia put her head on her knees, hiding her face behind her hair.

Doors slammed in the mansion above.

A sinking feeling hit Cassia. Someone else was definitely up there besides Kai. He didn't seem especially worried about it, which was a bad sign for Cassia.

And even if it was someone there to help Cassia, whoever it was probably was going to be too late to save her.

The top stair creaked with his weight as Kai stopped there. Cassia held her breath.

She could hear his panting inhales. He must have been running hard before he found the pantry.

How *had* he found the pantry?

Cassia clenched her eyes shut. Did it matter? She was going to die in this horrible hole in the ground.

He took one slow step after another down the stairs, swinging his phone light around the space as soon as he got low enough to duck beneath the ceiling and to look into it. Cassia pulled herself in even tighter.

The light passed along the walls and swept the floor inches from her feet. Cassia held her breath. She didn't dare move an inch. Even Miss Mansfield stayed perfectly still.

Stopping five steps from the bottom, Kai crouched and inspected the room from his perch.

He was inches from where she hid.

Cassia didn't move.

Seemingly satisfied, he turned on the stairs to go back up when the boards Cassia was leaning against cracked and moved a fraction of an inch.

The sound echoed in the close walls like a gunshot.

Kai stopped mid-step and slowly turned to face down the stairs again.

Blood pounded in Cassia's ears.

Suddenly Kai ran the rest of the way down the stairs, swinging the light as he landed to face Cassia where she huddled.

She scrambled to get away, but she was wedged in too tight.

"Don't move," he said, in a strange voice she'd never heard before.

He blasted his light in her face. Cassia tried to block the light with an arm, but it wasn't enough. The blinding whiteness stung her retinas. She turned away, blinking back tears.

"What do you want?" Cassia asked.

"I want what is mine. What that trash Mensky took from me. What I know you have." A thick, contemptuous rumble of a voice had replaced Kai's sunny surfer dude accent.

He sounded like the caricature of a rich person as seen on TV.

He sounded angry.

Mind spinning, Cassia tried to take in what he was saying. None of it made sense.

"I don't have anything," she finally said.

"What did Mensky put in your space?" Kai asked.

He knew about Mensky putting stuff in people's spaces?

"How did you know about that?" Cassia blurted out before she could stop herself.

Taking in a deep breath, he crouched down closer to Cassia, still directing the horrible light at her. He was a menacing black shadow behind it. "I've asked you once. I'm not going to keep asking."

The threat in his words hung in the air.

Miss Mansfield stepped between them and arched her back, hissing at Kai. The hiss continued to build into a ferocious wail as the cat drew closer to Kai. He swiped at Miss Mansfield, but the cat was faster, dashing out to attack with a slashing nail-tipped paw that left four bloody marks on Kai's arm.

He lowered the light as he raised a fist to smash the cat, but Cassia leaned in to block him. "No!"

The blow crashed down on Cassia's head, accompanied with the yawling of the cat behind her. The room felt dizzy and hot for a brief moment. Her ears rang.

A moment later, she tasted dirt as her head slowly sank to the floor.

Miss Mansfield howled, slashing again at Kai before making a dash up the stairs. Cassia felt a wave of irritation at the animal for abandoning her before the room went dark.

Cassia came to, still tasting dirt. At first, she thought it was one of her dreams of the red dirt of Mars, but the smell in her nostrils was too warm, too damp to be from any of her dreams.

It was the smell of the hidden basement in the Mandress Mansion.

She came fully awake with a start, only to feel a hand pressing down hard on her shoulder

And a gag in her mouth.

Kai had used his shirt to make a gag and torn strips to bind her arms. What she'd thought was a skinny young man was ripped, corded muscles. Even his face looked different in the harsh light of his phone.

He'd propped her up against the wall underneath the stairs, where he crouched down alongside her. Unless whoever was upstairs came all the way down, they'd never see them.

Voices drifted down from the kitchen.

"Ouch," came a faint exclamation.

More voices talking indistinctly. They were too far away. Despair pulled at Cassia.

"Ouch!" came a louder yell. "Dang nab cat!"

Sheriff Andrews! Genevieve must have called him!

Her eyes wide over the gag, Cassia turned to Kai. He held up one finger to his lips for her silence.

Forget that!

She immediately tried to yell, shaking her head to loosen the gag but it was too well tied.

Furious, Kai swung at Cassia's head.

Instead of waiting for the blow, Cassia flopped over on her side and kicked at Kai with both her heels aimed for his vulnerable tender spot exposed underneath his drawn up legs. Too late, he tried to defend himself.

She connected. Hard.

His scream echoed in the basement and up the stairs.

Feet came running.

Cassia rolled away on the dirt floor, getting out from under the stairs and into view of Sheriff Andrews and Deputy Chester as they came barrelling down the narrow stairs, their flashlights filling the space with light.

They looked around wildly. Cassia pointed with her feet at Kai.

Sheriff Andrews pulled Kai out by one leg, the man still clutching the family jewels.

Genevieve ran to Cassia and pulled down her gag.

"I was so worried, girl," Genevieve said as she grabbed Cassia in a bear hug.

"Me too," Cassia choked out, trying to ignore the tears streaming down her face. Genevieve hugged her again so tightly she was cutting off Cassia's windpipe. "Please…" Genevieve relaxed her grip enough for Cassia to say, "Please untie me."

Sheriff Andrews, Cassia, and Deputy Chester sat at the island in Cassia's kitchen while Genevieve put water in the tea kettle after having fed Miss Mansfield her reward for rescuing Cassia.

Cassia herself sat at the kitchen counter, staring dazedly ahead. It was just starting to sink in that she was safe.

Kai, the source of her trauma, sat in a chair off to one side, wearing one of Cassia's thrift store finds. It was a huge pink sweatshirt—one she'd come to hate—so it wasn't that painful to make him wear it. Plus the too-short sleeves made it easier to handcuff the jerk to the chair.

Sheriff Andrews held his notepad awkwardly, looking back and forth between Kai and Cassia. "So this was one of your hired movers—"

"Come on, dudes, this isn't really necessary," Kai said, his surfer accent magically back. He held up his handcuffed wrists, the chain between them clanking on the wooden arm of the chair.

Cassia glowered at him.

Not giving up without a fight, Kai protested, "I was just trying to help her."

Deputy Chester picked up one of the strips of fabric that had been used to tie Cassia up with the tip of his ballpoint pen. "This is helping?"

Both Cassia and Sheriff Andrews looked at the normally shy deputy in surprise. He shrugged his shoulders, his chin jutting in a stubborn way Cassia had never seen before.

"Oh come on. She wouldn't listen. *We* were supposed to be hiding from David. She totally misunderstood."

"I didn't misunderstand anything!" Cassia said, starting to get off her stool before Sheriff Andrews blocked her way. The sheriff stared at her in a considering way.

"Why didn't you come outside when we first pulled up?" Sheriff Andrews said. "We saw you run past the door."

"That was you?" Cassia asked, staring up at the Sheriff. She *should* have run out the door. Cassia snuck a glaring look at Miss Mansfield, who studiously ignored her while licking her tail.

"It was," Sheriff Andrews said.

"And the gunshot?" Cassia asked.

Sheriff Andrews cleared his throat while pointedly looking at Deputy Chester. Chester flushed and looked away while mumbling, "Saw something."

"Deer. You saw a deer," Sheriff Andrews said.

"At least I acted," Deputy Chester turned and said with a

rare flare of indignation that quickly evaporated under Sheriff Andrews withering glare.

"Dang it. I could have avoided all that." Cassia sat back down with a thump.

Sheriff Andrews paused, then set his notepad down in the kitchen island. "So, you can see how this is all a bit confusing."

"Wait, you aren't believing this guy, are you? How is it confusing?" Cassia asked, incredulous.

Sheriff Andrews and Deputy Chester didn't say anything.

Great.

How could they not believe her?

Cassia threw up her hands and looked around the kitchen. Some of the mess in the hallway caught her eye.

"Wait. I've got something to show you," Cassia said. She pushed past Sheriff Andrews and went to the hallway. Everything was still out there from her spill earlier, just messier, which was hard to believe. Digging under some papers, Cassia found what she was looking for.

She came back into the kitchen and shoved her find into Sheriff Andrews' hand. Genevieve tried to look over the sheriff's shoulder but he was too tall for her to see.

"What is this?" Sheriff Andrews said.

"A photograph," Deputy Chester said.

"I know that, you—" Sheriff Andrews in irritation, about to yell at Chester but stopping himself when he realized everyone was staring at him.

"Just like an old sitcom or something. Are you going to hit him with your hat too?" Genevieve asked Sheriff Andrews with a wink, almost daring him. At his gaping expression, she wormed her way into the circle to see what Cassia had brought back. "Oh, Senior Mandress when he was young."

"Yes, but that's not why I'm showing it," Cassia said.

"What else is there to see?" Deputy Chester asked, not as stubborn as Sheriff Andrews, who stared at the picture with a frown. That old goat would probably stare at it for an hour before he asked for help.

Well, Cassia wasn't feeling that patient.

"Not what, who," she said. She tapped on the photo. On the young man's face, the one with the blond swoop of hair across his forehead.

The one that looked like Kai had gone back in a time machine to the 1980s.

Deputy Chester and Genevieve leaned in to see what Cassia was pointing at.

Sheriff Andrews was the first to see it. "Oh," he said, understanding finally dawning.

Genevieve and Deputy Chester didn't take much longer.

As a group, they all slowly turned to stare at Kai.

CHAPTER 25

Kai sat in a chair off to one side in the huge open space of the kitchen, his pout and the ridiculous oversized pink sweatshirt Cassia had given the sheriff to cover the man just making him look like an overgrown six-year-old. Sheriff Andrews had run the handcuffs through the arm of the chair, so while Kai was sitting, he wasn't entirely comfortable, having to twist to one side.

Cassia almost felt sorry for him.

Almost.

Who knows what he would have done to her if she hadn't gotten the attention of the others one floor above her? She might have died in the tiny room in the basement.

She repressed a shudder. It already felt like a coffin down there. It was no good to think that it might have really become hers.

Sheriff Andrews led the group over to stand in front of Kai. Cassia found her way around the chairs circling the island to join Genevieve and Deputy Chester standing next to the sheriff.

They all stared at Kai.

Kai broke first. "What?" he asked, the question almost a shriek.

"Who is this man?" Sheriff Andrews said, holding the photograph out for Kai to see.

Kai barely glanced down at it. "How should I know, man?" he said.

"Try again," Sheriff Andrews said, his voice quiet and calm. Deadly calm. He held the photo upright in front of Kai.

Reluctantly, Kai turned his eyes to the photograph and examined its contents. His eyes flicked back and forth. A flush rose up on his cheeks.

"You know who that is, right?" Cassia said, pushing forward. "You know, because that's your father. Admit it!"

Now everyone stared at Cassia. "What? The guy looks just like Kai."

"That jerk is not my father," Kai said, his voice clear and ringing. The surfer persona gone again just like that.

Sheriff Andrews' eyebrows shot up.

"Don't *ever* say that guy was my father," Kai said again. He tried to draw himself up with some dignity, but the handcuffs wouldn't let him. Or the hot pink sweatshirt, for that matter.

"Looks like it could be your father," Genevieve said. Cassia caught the intentional provocation, but one glance at Sheriff Andrews and Deputy Chester showed they hadn't. Either that or they had better poker faces than Cassia did.

Big surprise there. Cassia could barely keep words from flying out of her mouth, much less keeping what she really thought off of her face.

"Who is it, if it isn't your father?" Cassia asked, sick of waiting for Kai to take the bait and explain himself.

"Otto Huntington. My viperous uncle," Kai said, almost spitting the words with disgust.

The group took that in. It wasn't hard to believe that Kai was related to the man in the photograph. They looked so nearly identical.

After staring back down at the photograph again, Genevieve gave a soft gasp. "It looks," Genevieve said as she took the photo from Sheriff Andrews, "like they are with Owen Mensky."

Owen Mensky? The dead, crabby-as-all-get-out storage space caretaker?

Cassia grabbed the photo from Genevieve. The face was rounder, and the stomach flatter, but those eyes were the same. And the same disgusting cigar hung out of his mouth. It looked as soggy and chewed as the one he'd had when he'd yelled at Cassia about who she was letting into her rental space. Cassia could almost smell the wet tobacco and the faint odor of mildew.

"How old is this photo?" Cassia asked.

"Probably thirty years old," Genevieve said, startling Cassia. Cassia hadn't really expected an answer.

Genevieve took the photo back. "Senior Mandress looks about sixty, maybe seventy. And the other two look like they were college kids. I'm guessing Owen Mensky was in his fifties when he died."

Unable to help herself, Cassia glanced to Sheriff Andrews for confirmation. He nodded.

"Do you know where this photo was taken?" Cassia asked Kai.

For an answer, Kai twisted away from her, letting her stare at the pink expanse of his back while he stared at the nearby wall.

She recognized that answer from Miss Mansfield. He wasn't going to say another word on his own.

Dang it.

Genevieve and Cassia sat over their third cups of hot cocoa in the kitchen. The dawn had come and gone and now late morning sunshine came in the back windows. Cassia knew she should get some sleep. Her head felt woozy and dizzy with exhaustion, and the cocoa barely masked the sleep-deprived nausea, but going to bed meant Genevieve would leave, which meant being alone in the mansion again.

Not something she was ready for just yet.

Cassia had never done well with being isolated, and having a mansion in the middle of nowhere *and* getting attacked was doing nothing good for her anxiety.

"It's nice that Sheriff Andrews is letting you come and make a statement after getting some sleep," Genevieve said. The sheriff and deputy had taken their charge away. They had enough to hold him for at least a day.

"Ha!" Cassia said. "He probably wanted to get some sleep himself."

Genevieve yawned. "Can you blame him?"

"Did you notice how perfectly pressed his uniform was?" Cassia stirred the bottom dregs of chocolate in her cup. "It was the freaking middle of the night, and he looked like it was noon on a Tuesday."

Genevieve glanced at the enormous clock. "It is almost noon on a Tuesday."

"You know what I mean. The man is like a robot in some ways." Cassia could barely pull herself together on a normal day. How could that man respond to an emergency in the middle of the night and still be so professional in all ways? His pants still had crisp lines from ironing, for heaven's sake!

It both irritated her, and made her jealous, if she was to be honest.

"You know, this photo doesn't look like it is in the US. Those buildings look so old." Genevieve stared at the photo. They'd searched for more photographs in the rest of the stuff in the hall and hadn't found another like it. Or even a note about it.

"It could be New York," Cassia said, laying her head down on her arms. Maybe she'd just shut her eyes for a few minutes in the kitchen. "There's graffiti in the background. Isn't there a lot of graffiti and old buildings in New York?"

"Um, maybe." Genevieve peered closer, the photo almost touching her nose. "There is graffiti but it's weird... I can't understand what it says."

Cassia closed her eyes, almost drifting off when Genevieve slapped the table.

"No way!" Genevieve said. "Cassia, you're a genius."

"I am?" Cassia lifted her head and peered at Genevieve blearily.

"For noticing the graffiti. It's there all right. It looks weird because it's in German. That photo was taken in Germany!" Genevieve shoved the photo to Cassia as she pulled out her phone and did a search.

"Ah ha! This looks just like that section of wall." Genevieve held up a photo with tall sections of concrete broken apart and leaning back, some lying on the ground like fallen dominos. "This was what the German wall looked like before it came down. I bet you anything that photo was in Berlin."

Genevieve spun around and did a happy dance in the kitchen, not at all looking like she'd been up all night.

Cassia stared across Sheriff Andrew's desk at the man himself. She'd managed to get some sleep that afternoon, but still felt like she'd been run over by a Mack truck. He, of course, looked perfect. Which just made her madder than the news he gave.

"What do you mean, you can't press charges? What changed since this morning?"

"We need some proof. Right now it's his word against yours. And we still haven't found David Clyders." Sheriff Andrews rubbed his forehead, exhaustion showing for the first time. "And it's come out at least twenty people saw David barrelling down Main Street the other day, acting erratically and putting people in danger. Another dozen have had run-ins with the guy. It's completely conceivable Kai was trying to protect you from him."

Cassia crossed her arms. "He was not."

Sheriff Andrews leaned back and crossed his own arms. "I need proof."

They stared at each other. Off on the other side of the room, Deputy Chester glanced over anxiously from his own desk. The atmosphere of the station felt thick and tense.

"So you're just going to let him go?" Cassia asked.

"I don't have a choice if there is no proof. He's only still here because I've not known you to lie yet." He leaned forward and tapped the desk in front of Cassia. "But it's not in your favor he was the one screaming when we found you guys, not you."

"Because I was tied up!" Cassia barely kept herself from yelling it at him.

"Well, you don't always do the smartest things."

Oh no, he so did not.

Was he *blaming her* for misunderstanding Kai? No. That was no misunderstanding. Kai was not protecting her from anything, least of all himself.

White-hot fire obscured Cassia's vision. She had to get out of there before she said something she really would regret.

Without risking a single word, Cassia rose from her seat and bolted from the station.

She thought she could hear Kai laughing from the cell around the corner. She tried to slam the station door on the way out, but the air brake slowed it too much. Giving up, she stomped down the street.

What a no-good, rotten day.

CHAPTER 26

Cassia watched Genevieve pile the whipped cream onto a slice of walnut tort. The caramel-covered walnuts and toasted crust disappeared under a pile of fluffy white. All too soon Genevieve reached the bottom of the bowl, scraping for the last bits of beaten cream. Looking around and then holding a finger to her lips, Genevieve signaled for Cassia to not say a word, then walked to the tall cooler in the back corner and grabbed another full bowl of whipped cream. Pulling back the film, she dug in a large serving spoon and piled more good stuff on Cassia's plate.

Genevieve gave Cassia a conspiratorial smile before putting the film back on the bowl and stowing it back in the cooler.

Cassia eyed the dessert in awe. The plate was barely visible beneath the pile of whipped cream atop it. The slice of tort, huge in its own right, was completely hidden. Cassia's mouth watered at the deliciousness awaiting her.

"You know food doesn't make things right?" Cassia said. She tried for a cavalier attitude, but even she couldn't pull it off with so much yumminess waiting for her.

"No, but it makes things better," Genevieve said. She

pushed the plate over the counter to Cassia and handed her a fork.

Cassia needed no further instructions.

Her fork clinked on the plate in the quietness of the diner. It was past dinnertime and the locals had gotten used to the diner closing early in the winter months. Luckily the doors had still been open when Cassia had come by since Trent was doing some deep cleaning in the back and Genevieve had not yet closed up the front.

The diner felt like a second home at this point, almost better than her main one, since there were people there who cared about her. Miss Mansfield was nice, but it was hard to just have a cat for company.

About halfway through the tort, the tension behind Cassia's eyes eased and she felt the blood flowing freely again. When she'd finished, the white-hot rage she'd felt when she'd walked in the door was replaced by a feeling of wellness and satisfaction, with only a twinge of pain from her gut stretching with the huge serving. That was a good sort of pain Cassia could handle every day of the week.

"Better?" Genevieve asked as she came by with a pot of decaf coffee and poured Cassia a cup.

Cassia nodded.

"So, you need evidence," Genevieve said as she put the coffee pot back in its holder. "Let's see what we can do." She lifted the counter to come around and sat on a stool next to Cassia.

Pulling out her waitress pad, Genevieve tore off two sheets and gave one to Cassia, along with one of her pens.

"How long do you have?" Genevieve asked.

Cassia shrugged. She'd not thought to ask.

"Let's see," Genevieve said as she pulled out her phone and did a quick search. "Minnesota law says thirty-six hours max without getting a judge's order. What did Sheriff Andrews say?"

Nothing good, Cassia thought bitterly.

She glanced at Genevieve's waiting eyes. Yeah, that didn't answer the question. "I better ask," Cassia said as she pulled out her own phone and pulled up the number for the sheriff's office. The fact that it was a number Cassia should not have had programmed in her phone was not lost on her. She never would have been able to predict the last few weeks if a thousand monkeys had been typing possible events for millennia.

No one could. It was all just too weird.

"*Sheriff's office,*" Sheriff Andrews said into the phone. Holy cannolis, he answered the phone himself.

"Um, hi, Sheriff Andrews, it's Cassia."

"I know."

"Yeah, well, how long do I have to give you evidence? I forgot to ask," Cassia said, refusing to acknowledge that she'd stormed out of his office. Or tried to.

"*You did seem to be in somewhat of a hurry,*" he said, a strange tone in his voice.

Was he laughing at her?

"Yes, well, please just answer my question." Cassia said stiffly. She wasn't finding humor in any of this.

"*Thirty-six hours. He has to go before Judge Smith tomorrow morning at the latest to be held any longer. That's the law,*" Sheriff Andrews said, his tone back to the no-nonsense flatness Cassia had come to expect from the man.

"I'd never expect you to break the law," Cassia said hotly.

"*Good to hear,*" Sheriff Andrews said, followed by the line dropping to silence.

Cassia squeezed her eyes shut and pulled in memories of the tart she'd just eaten as her version of calming meditation. It helped. She opened them to find Genevieve staring at her.

"Thirty-six hours, just as you said. Tomorrow morning he

has to go in front of the judge," Cassia said. Or go free, something Cassia didn't even want to say out loud.

Genevieve nodded. She glanced at the plate windows facing Main Street. The few cars parked along the street were only dim shadows in the fading light. "Trying to find David seems like a fool's errand if the sheriff and Trent can't get a hold of him. We don't have much time," Genevieve said.

"Right," Cassia said. She flicked her pen on the counter, trying to think where they could find more evidence. Some of the boxes back at the storage space? Or at the mansion?

The mansion.

Cassia nudged Genevieve. "How did Kai know where I lived?"

Genevieve made a small "o" with her mouth. Somehow no one had asked Kai that question. Not that Cassia expected an honest answer from the guy.

"It was David's phone that was stuck in the truck outside the mansion, and now no one can find the guy..." Genevieve said, staring off into the distance as if imagining all the bad endings David could have come to. Cassia could think of a few on her own.

"If David's phone was used to locate the mansion, do you think Kai did something to him to get that information?"

Genevieve shook her head. "David wasn't exactly great about contacting Trent back from the start. It could just be a coincidence."

"Or it isn't, and Mensky isn't the only dead body."

"Cassia! Let's not go there. At least not right away," Genevieve said, her eyebrows pinched together in concern. Considering how unfazed Genevieve was by most things, Cassia took that as a not great sign.

Thirty minutes and two cups of coffee later, Cassia and Genevieve had a few items on their lists to check. Since time was so short, they were going to have to split up. The plan was for Cassia to search the mansion, Genevieve to check the storage space, and Roger to meet them pre-dawn with whatever he found overnight.

Genevieve looked at Cassia and gave her a wink as she talked to Roger on her cell phone, finalizing the plans. "Right, so unless we hear otherwise, we'll meet you in the storage space parking lot at 4 am. Do we need to bring anything?"

Cassia could not hear the mumbled response coming from the other end.

"That's a good idea, but where?"

Another pause.

Grabbing their mugs, Cassia rounded the counter and put them inside the bus bin.

"Right. Call us with the location then." Genevieve hung up her phone.

"What location?" Cassia asked.

"Roger thinks he might have figured out the map. He's using some street view stuff to triangulate it. Plus he mentioned our cars—definitely yours—are known. Parking in the storage space parking lot might not be the safest thing right now if Kai really is the innocent one in all this."

Cassia grimaced. He wasn't wrong.

"Roger that," Cassia said. She held up her list. "I'm off. Keep your phone charged."

"You too," Genevieve said as she grabbed her backpack and keys from under the counter. They were off to find evidence. "Be careful at the mansion," Genevieve said.

Cassia nodded and was out the door.

Twenty-six miles later, Cassia wasn't feeling so brave. The danger posed by a mouse in the kitchen was laughable compared to the possible danger that could come from a lurking man with an ax to grind. A shiver ran through Cassia. That wasn't a good image right now.

No axes.

No lurking men.

She focused on seeing Miss Mansfield's waiting furry face. If Miss Mansfield was waiting inside the entryway, things were probably okay.

If Miss Mansfield wasn't waiting there, Cassia was planning on making a run for the car and joining Genevieve at the storage space.

Despite it only being a little past 7 pm, the twisting road leading up to the mansion was dark and foreboding. The broken branches from Cassia's initial foray with her moving van still poked out over the road. Getting tree trimmers in had been low on her list of priorities.

Not even considering driving back to the rear of the house and into the woods where the garage stood, Cassia pulled around the front roundabout and parked her car at a crazy angle so her driver's door was close to the front door. Yes, she'd have to drive over some grass to make a getaway, but at least she wouldn't waste precious seconds running around the car.

She'd seen too many horror movies to make that mistake.

Also, she wasn't stupid enough to go into dark basements on her own, like the heroines of those movies always did.

Or was she?

Cassia pushed out the memory of hiding from Kai from her mind. That was different. She was trying to get away from the horrible guy, not investigate.

Cassia parked the car and turned off the engine. Every light in the mansion was off. Cassia groaned. She was going to have to get some light timers, or a just leave a few lights on from now on, because coming home to this was just too much.

She knew that if she was in a movie, right about now the audience would be yelling at her to leave before whatever bad person was waiting came out to get her.

Cassia shook herself. She was letting her imagination run away. More than likely, the real bad guy was locked in downtown Forbidden Valley, counting the hours until he could be free again to terrorize her for whatever thing he imagined she had.

Kai's voice—his real voice—had been terrifying. Whatever he wanted, he wanted it badly. Badly enough to do terrible things. One night in jail wasn't going to stop him.

No. Cassia had to find the evidence to stop him for longer, and for good.

Creeping up to the front stoop, Cassia tried to peer into the windows that bracketed the front door, but she couldn't see anything. It was just as dark in there as it was outside, if not darker.

Taking a deep breath, Cassia put her key in the lock Rodger had fixed for her earlier and jiggled the handle to allow the bolt to be retracted and turned the key.

It all sounded so horribly loud in the oppressive darkness.

She slowly opened the door and waited.

CHAPTER 27

Cassia stood in front of the front door of the mansion, listening. It was such an old house that there were no light switches close to the door. One had to enter and walk in far enough to turn on one of the table lamps on the narrow side tables that flanked the entryway.

Something Cassia was not going to do unless she got the all clear, which so far had not come.

Inside, pitch darkness matched the pitch darkness of the night behind her. Cassia had not appreciated the city comfort of always having lights on until now. Street lights, traffic lights, house lights.

All things that were most definitely not here.

Only a dark mansion, a dark night sky, and dark woods surrounding the whole deal.

It was enough to give a young woman gray hair.

Holding vigil by the door, Cassia gripped her keys tightly, ready to bolt at the first unexpected sound.

Just as she couldn't take it anymore, the faint padding of paws on polished wood came echoing down the hall. A long, piercing meow followed.

That was definitely Miss Mansfield.

Exhaling, Cassia felt light-headed. She hadn't realized she'd been holding her breath until she started breathing again.

Miss Mansfield ran up and rubbed against Cassia's legs.

"Oh, I'm so happy to see you too," Cassia said.

Another loud, demanding meow was the only response.

Cassia entered the house, shut and locked the door behind her, and then turned on every light she could reach as she followed Miss Mansfield back to the kitchen.

The mansion now blazed brightly like a Christmas tree owned by the richest people in three states. She'd run through the place, turning on every light switch she could find. She told herself it was to make her search for evidence quicker and faster, but Cassia knew it was really because the light felt comforting and safe.

She might be out there alone, but anyone coming up the drive would think there was an army afoot in the place.

The library had been her first choice, but it had only taken a few moments for Cassia to change her mind about that. The books in the library might be a good place for her aunt to leave her secret notes, but she needed to find out more about Senior Mandress and where he might have been thirty years ago. Published textbooks would have no clue on that, at least none she could think of.

So Cassia dragged out every last banker's box she and Genevieve had moved in from the truck. Some of them, most of them most likely, were Senior Mandress's papers. There had to be something in there.

In the very last box, under a pile of seemingly random newspaper clippings in different languages, Cassia found what she was looking for; a hand-typed manuscript entitled

"Galactic Collisions and Their Consequences", credited with work done at Effelsberg 100-m Radio Telescope in Bonn Germany and thanks to a grant from Senior Mandress, along with a handwritten note of thanks.

The note was written by Owen Mensky.

Cassia almost choked when she read the signature on the note. Owen Mensky?

Grabbing the typed paper, she checked the authorship. Owen Mensky was the first author.

No way.

Somehow, Cassia felt a shred of pity for the man. As unpleasant as he'd been, finding out that he had at one time shared one of her passions put him in a whole different light. Not an entirely good light, but still better than what little she'd known of him before.

So that *had* been Owen Mensky in the photograph. What a strange and weird coincidence to run into him at the Mucho Junk.

Or had it been a coincidence?

A shudder ran through Cassia. What on earth was going on?

Even at 4 am, a hint of pink edged the eastern sky when the horizon showed between the thick pine trees. Cassia yawned as she steered her car slowly through the twisting roads. It was deer season, and she was not going to crash her new-to-her car on some animal's furry face. Bad for the animal. Worse for Cassia's bank account.

She'd briefly debated taking a nap or having more coffee

back at the mansion when the clock had struck 2 am, but decided she could sleep after they'd gained their evidence, because she couldn't imagine sleeping well otherwise.

Finally, her phone pinged that she'd arrived at her destination. She looked around in confusion. It was the edge of thick woods fronting highway 71 a few miles from the storage space. Besides a narrow gravel pad, there was little to recommend it as a destination.

How had Roger even been able to send her an address to get to this spot?

A few moments later, Roger's van turned the corner, followed by Genevieve's blue car. She could ask the man himself.

But that didn't happen. Roger nearly exploded out of the van, glee written all over his normally calm face. Cassia had never seen him look like that, not even over Fish Fry Friday at the diner. The man was practically on the moon in happiness.

"What happened?" Cassia asked.

"I'm a genius," Roger said as he rounded his van and threw the back door open to grab his metal detector. Cassia watched him open-mouthed, eliciting a laugh from Genevieve now standing outside her own car.

"Do you know what's going on?" Cassia asked.

"I do, but that would be telling," Genevieve said, giving Cassia an infuriating wink. Genevieve grabbed the second metal detector on the van bed and followed Roger off into the woods.

Cassia put her hands on her hips and frowned.

The only good thing was that, judging by Roger's haste, she'd have her answer soon enough.

"One hundred twenty-one," Roger said, taking huge strides and counting each one, "one hundred twenty-two, one hundred twenty-three. There, that's it." He looked around at the clearing. It looked identical to the last hundred paces of woods. Snapping his compass shut, he slid it into his pocket.

Not waiting for instructions, Genevieve swiped her metal detector along the base of the trees surrounding the open spot where Roger stood.

"I thought that detector didn't get deep enough?" Cassia asked, pointing at Genevieve, and confused at the whole situation.

"Ah, but our mapmakers were clever. It's part of the map," Roger said.

Cassia was starting to get really irritated with both of them. She was the one who had been assaulted. She should know what was going on.

As if sensing her darkening mood, Roger relented.

"There are supposed to be near-surface markers. They're to be used to triangulate the final location."

Um, what?

Ding Ding. Genevieve's detector went off. A few trowels of dirt later, Genevieve held a large silver coin high. "A 1938 French 20 franc," Genevieve called. She and Roger exchanged looks.

"Cat," Genevieve said. Cassia turned warily to her. She'd noticed Genevieve used her nickname a lot when she was about to ask for a particularly unpleasant favor. "Can you go back to the van and get the posthole digger? We might need it in a few minutes. Also, there is a box in the back of my car that I found in the storage space that might be important."

Cassia flinched but still managed to catch the keys Genevieve threw to her. She gritted her teeth at the thought of walking through the dark woods alone, but lit up her phone's flashlight and went off without a word.

She'd get Genevieve back one of these days. There had to be a way.

Cassia found the posthole digger on a sheet of plastic in the back of Roger's van, which thankfully he'd not bothered to lock.

Curious as to what Genevieve's box was, Cassia decided to investigate that before making the trek back lugging the ridiculously heavy piece of equipment. Honestly, she should have refused the task unless someone else came with her.

The box in the back of Genevieve's car was one of the easily identifiable banker's boxes. Lifting the lid, Cassia saw a chaotic mess of newspaper clippings, giving her an idea of what the rest of the storage space probably looked like.

But at least Genevieve thought she'd found something.

Picking up one of the yellowed clippings, Cassia checked the date. 1989. At least these clippings of long narrow columns of text were all in English.

One word ran through them repeatedly. *Gold*. The word *Nazi* and *USSR* made close seconds.

Pushing the box further into the car, Cassia sat on the seat next to it and tried to make sense of all the articles it held.

"Cassia! We've been waiting for you!" Genevieve called.

Cassia looked up, her eyes struggling to focus. The light filtered through the pines and leaf bare deciduous trees. It was past sunrise. How long had she been reading?

"Sorry, I just..."

"Found the box," Genevieve finished for her. "I think

you're going to like what we've found even more. If we can get it up out of the ground."

That was a stiff promise. Cassia shoved the article in her hand back into the box and scrambled out of the car. Together she and Genevieve hauled the heavy post-hole digger from Roger's truck, along with a few shovels, back into the woods.

CHAPTER 28

"I don't like this," Sheriff Andrews said, staring at Roger, Cassia, and Genevieve as they stood outside the sheriff's station. Cassia had managed to convince him to come outside. He was already irate when Cassia had called to ask him to wait until the last minute to let Kai go.

Cassia crossed her own arms. It was easy enough to do in the chill air. Maybe it was the cold, or her exhaustion, or the sheer weight of being in danger too many times in too few weeks, but she was feeling more anger and less fear of the staunch rule-following man.

It's not as if what she was asking was illegal.

"It's too dangerous," Sheriff Andrews said.

"Isn't that for me to decide?" Cassia asked.

He merely huffed at her.

"Isn't it more dangerous for Kai to go free to come after me later?" Cassia said, pressing her point home.

They glared at each other.

"Fine." Sheriff Andrews threw up his hands and walked back into the station.

Cassia glanced at Roger and Genevieve, who gave her

thumbs-up. Her victory smile fell a bit when she realized now she just had to do the thing.

Kai looked up when Deputy Chester came to the cell door with the big ring of keys and Cassia following close behind.

"Coming to thank me for rockin' saving your life?" Kai asked, the California accent thick. Cassia had to give him credit. Even after more than twenty-four hours in that awful cell, he was sticking to his story. Cassia did not have good memories of her own time in that cell.

"Something like that," Cassia said as she entered the cell and nodded at Deputy Chester. Hesitating a moment, Deputy Chester locked the cell and walked back to his desk just around the corner. He would be able to hear them well enough, even if they weren't in direct eyeline.

The only place to sit was the narrow cot where Kai himself sat. It didn't look like he'd slept at all, the thick green army blanket still pulled tightly across the bed.

Seeing her gaze, Kai made room for her and patted the cot next to him. Taking in a deep breath, Cassia went over to sit by the man.

He looked no worse for wear. Only the faintest of bruises by his temple spoke of the struggle he'd had with Sheriff Andrews on Monday night.

"I do want to thank you for letting me know there was something going on," Cassia began, struggling to find the right words. Somehow, on the outside, she'd thought talking would be the easy part.

Kai narrowed his eyes.

"Such as?"

"Oh, you know, the dangers of being a woman alone in that big mansion," Cassia added, leaving off the second part of

that sentence in her head, which was mostly about the impor-
tance of avoiding creepers like Kai.

A smarmy smile crept up Kai's face. "Glad to be of service
to my fine lady o' the north." He gave her a hang-five wiggle
of his thumb and pinky finger.

Cassia was starting to hate that gesture. Especially when
that creepy smile meant he took her words to mean she was
now scared.

Looking down, Cassia forced herself to recenter and not be
distracted by how much she wanted to kick this guy in the
shins. Or elsewhere.

"Yes, well, I wanted to stop by to give my thanks in
person before you left. I imagine you're eager to get back out
west and to the warm sunshine," Cassia said. "In any case, I
don't have your contact information since I only have
David's"

She leaned in to him, lowering her voice. "They still
haven't found David. Do you know where he is?"

He tilted his head at her question, unsure of her intent.

Right. Wrong track.

Rushing on so he wouldn't think about her last remarks too
much, Cassia went on. "Um, sorry, I guess you would have said
something if you knew since he was so dangerous and all that.
Nevermind."

Cassia dug in her pants pocket, fumbling with a folded
piece of paper and accidentally pulling out the other contents
of her pocket, which was a sparkling 1931 gold British
sovereign. It rolled on the jail cell floor past Kai's feet. His eyes
fixated on it. He sprang from his seat and slapped the coin
down, leaving the cot wobbling and almost sending Cassia to
the floor.

Kai hunched over the coin, reminding Cassia of Sméagol
from *The Lord of the Rings*. He turned back to face Cassia, his
expression horrifying.

"A 1931 M sovereign. I knew you had them, you lying wench," he hissed. No trace of California sunshine.

Only black, black hatred.

"I don't know what you're talking about. That's my lucky coin. My aunt left it for me as part of the will."

Not even getting up from the floor, he turned and crawled towards Cassia. Her neck itched. She scrambled from the cot and ran to the cell bars, hitting them with a clang as she turned back to face Kai.

He rose and stalked toward her. "That is not *your* lucky coin. That is my coin. That is one of the coins that bastard Otto stole using my father's research."

"Your father?" Cassia asked. She had to get more information, and quickly.

"My father, Wolfram Huntington, the famed Soviet researcher, who knew where they'd hidden the gold."

"Who? What gold?" Cassia asked.

Kai reached Cassia and stood inches from her face, trapping her against the bars. She closed her eyes. "What gold?" she asked again weakly.

"The Soviet special forces. The gold they'd stolen and then stashed in Eastern Germany." The spray of his spit on her eyelids sent Cassia's stomach into spasms.

His breath was awful.

She had no doubt if he wasn't in jail at that moment, he'd be strangling her.

He went on, leaning closer to speak in her ear. "The gold that sleazeball Mensky took, and somehow gave to you. Give it back to its rightful owner and save yourself. It's not too late."

"It is for you," Sheriff Andrews said, flinging the jail cell open with a bang and pulling Kai off Cassia by the collar of his sweatshirt.

Cassia sank to the jail floor, her heart trying to escape her body.

"Are you alright?" Genevieve asked as she handed Cassia a cup of hot cocoa. Deputy Chester had helped Cassia walk to his desk and then found a thick blanket to wrap around her shoulders.

Cassia had no idea where Genevieve had found the hot cocoa, but it was more than welcome.

Sheriff Andrews and Kai were off at the courthouse. Roger had tagged along with them, mostly to hear what Kai said for himself. Cassia was glad he'd be there to witness it, since she knew Sheriff Andrews to be tight-lipped about any investigations, even if they involved her.

After several minutes in the quiet sheriff's station, Cassia felt she could breathe again. The sugar from the cocoa flowed through her blood and the world seemed reasonable again.

It was also definitely safer than it had been half an hour ago, at least for her.

"How did you know he would say anything?" Genevieve asked.

"I didn't know for sure," Cassia said as she put the empty cup down on Deputy Chester's desk. "He wasn't really that great an actor, and tormenting him with having that coin wasn't really fair, was it?" She gave a weak laugh.

"It is a beautiful coin," Genevieve admitted. They'd lucked out in that the first one they tried cleaning was a perfect specimen. Enough to make a greedy man lose his cool.

"Besides," Cassia said, "I was also banking on him being just like his uncle, or his father, the famed researcher. Half those newspaper articles interviewed the man and he couldn't stop bragging about how much he knew about soviet history this and soviet history that and what an exciting time it was that the east was opening up again. I just had a hunch if a map with soviet symbols led us to gold, he would know something about it. He and his nephew Kai.”

“But why would Senior Mandress have kept those articles?” Genevieve asked. “It’s got nothing to do with astronomy.”

Cassia shrugged. “I dunno. Maybe because Otto was Owen Mensky’s friend? Maybe because he liked historical events?”

She turned away from Genevieve. Once again, life was reminding her of just how little she knew her family members, especially the ones the most like her, and if there was any justice in the world, the ones she should know the best. It was the worst thing ever that she’d never met her grandfather or aunt, not even once.

Not that she knew of anyhow.

As if sensing her mood, Genevieve rubbed Cassia’s back.

CHAPTER 29

"Wow, another party," Roger said as he passed by Genevieve and Cassia talking by the diner counter. He grabbed a handful of fish-shaped crackers from the bowl set in with all the other pre-dinner snacks. "Is this what rich people do? Throw parties all the time?"

Cassia laughed awkwardly. She was not rich, and at the rate she was going she never would be.

Roger went to a booth where they'd set up a punch bowl and helped himself to some pink punch with lemon slices floating in it. It was early yet. He'd shown up when Cassia and Genevieve were still hanging the paper chains and cutout turkeys in the windows. It could not have looked more like something a six-year-old had done, and Cassia loved it.

A few of the townsfolk drifted in the front door, setting the bells ringing. Some carried dishes, others dropped a few dollars in the donation bowl set on the front hostess stand for those less fortunate.

If everyone arrived, almost every seat in the diner would be full. Cassia felt giddy. Even Sheriff Andrews and Deputy Chester and his girlfriend were coming.

This party was her idea, or rather it had started out as being hers.

Actually, Genevieve had made it all happen. When she'd heard that it'd been years since Cassia had been at a real Thanksgiving dinner, she talked Trent into hosting dinner at the diner. The mansion was still a mess with moving stuff in from the storage space, and besides, Cassia had never cooked a turkey in her life.

And she still hadn't caught that dang mouse. She did not want any company seeing *that* in her house.

"I still don't understand why we can't microwave the bird? Microwaves are so much faster than ovens," Cassia said, pushing away thoughts of rodents. Her stomach growled for the third time in an hour. She looked longingly at the appetizers but refused to spoil her dinner.

"And that," Genevieve said as she pushed Cassia toward the punch, "is why you are not cooking tonight. We are having a traditional Thanksgiving dinner with *roast* Turkey."

"What about vegetarians?" Cassia asked. "Do they get to microwave their dinners and eat sooner?"

Genevieve stared at Cassia, her eyebrows nearly at her hairline. "I swear, you are worse than my brother as a kid. Does your brain short-circuit when you're hungry?"

"No," Cassia said with a pout. She turned to the punch bowl and grabbed a cup to ladle some for herself. "Maybe." She said under her breath when facing away from Genevieve.

"Ha! I heard that," Genevieve said.

"What?" Cassia asked innocently. "I think you need to clean your ears out." She walked off in a fake huff. Nate had just walked in, or rather ducked to get in the front door, and she wanted to for-real bug him about her New York accounts and maybe getting some money. Or some reward money.

Something more than a few hundred here and a few

hundred there that her aunt seemed to have enjoyed spreading about.

Nate Perauski and his tiny wife, Madison, added their coats to the pile in the small half-booth by the wall. When they turned back to the room, Cassia was waiting.

"Hi!" she said with an overenthusiastic smile and a wave.

She was dang lucky Nate didn't run and hide every time he saw her coming, not that there were many places to hide a seven-foot-tall man. She was always bugging him for money.

It wasn't her fault a mansion was such an expensive place to run.

Or even just pay for some light.

"Hey, Cassia, how does it feel to be famous?" Madison asked. "I kept a copy of the Countryside Journal just so I can show people who my husband works with. The smart girl who figures out mysteries and finds stolen gold."

Heat flushed Cassia's face. "Oh, I didn't do all that. Roger was the one that figured out the map. Besides, now people are going to be bugging me about getting some gold."

"No, they won't," Nate said. "We've learned our lesson and every article now carefully says all the gold is getting returned back overseas so the rightful owners can be tracked down. Though, I must say, I still can't believe they are still finding spoils from World War 2. And here, of all places."

Cassia fully agreed. She'd not thought about how alarming it would be to have people think you were rich until Kai had come after her for all the gold he thought she'd had. Luckily, Nate was a very competent and persistent lawyer who also had a way with journalists.

A throat cleared behind Cassia. She turned to see who it was.

"Speaking of finding spoils," Trent said. He stood in front of the swinging doors that led back to the kitchen with an arm draped around an abashed David Clyders. "Look who I found lurking around the back door."

"He wasn't lurking," Genevieve said in a no-nonsense tone as she grabbed David's arm and pulled him further into the diner. "He was invited. The least we could do is feed the guy a turkey dinner after he was tied up in an apartment basement for three days because it didn't occur to us that he was in real trouble."

Taking his coat, Genevieve pushed David to the punch bowl. It must be her go-to move to make people happy. *Here, have some sugar.*

Not a bad move, Cassia had to concede.

They had all felt pretty bad when a 911 call about animals in an apartment basement turned out to be David Clyders tied up to a chair and flopping around to make as much noise as possible. Kai had intended to come back and let him go after getting the goods from Cassia, but that plan had taken a detour into Sheriff Andrews' jail cell.

Holding a tiny punch cup, David circled around and stood awkwardly in front of Cassia. Nate and Madison took the hint and drifted off to the appetizer table.

Cassia stared at David, then looked around nervously before glancing back at him.

"What—" Cassia started.

"Sorry about Kai," David blurted out. "He was a bad employee. I had no idea about the phone thing. He just said he needed to use my phone because he didn't have one. I didn't know he left it in the truck on purpose."

"Didn't say a word about using it to track where I lived, did he?" Cassia asked, unable to stop herself from teasing the man a little.

"No. Sorry." He looked down at his shoes.

Dang it, now Cassia felt bad.

"It's okay, don't worry about it," Cassia said.

His eyes didn't move.

"You can move the rest of my stuff out of the storage space into the mansion."

David looked up excitedly.

"—but you need better help. That's a requirement." Cassia held up one finger.

He nodded.

Cassia sighed, then put her arm in his and led him back to the group now laying out plates for the main meal.

Trent had promised turkey at 7 pm sharp and Cassia was ready for it.

ABOUT THE AUTHOR

Shaw Collins is owned by another perfect Miss Mansfield and lives in the frozen tundra of the upper Midwest whilst dreaming of warm summer nights.

ALSO BY SHAW COLLINS

CASSIA LEMON MYSTERIES

Cat on a Wire

Cat Dancer

Cat and Mouse

www.ShawCollins.com